To:
Jeannine

Lori Michael
Janice Grembowski

Lighthouse Love
And Secrets

By

Lori Michael

PublishAmerica
Baltimore

First printing

ISBN: 1-4137-0354-2
PUBLISHED BY PUBLISHAMERICA, LLLP
www.publishamerica.com
Baltimore

Printed in the United States of America

This book is dedicated to my family.
They will always be an important part of my life.

Also to a very special friend who has always been there for me
and encouraged me to pursue my dream of writing.
If you think you are that friend, you are.

CHAPTER 1

It has been almost a year since I have been on this boat or even considered taking it out. I had watched Brian so many times as he prepared to take to the open waters. It all seemed so easy for him. Now it was up to me to do this myself. Helen and Reggie were there to help me, but I needed to try this alone. My goal was to be able to take the boat out by myself to see a sunrise or sunset whenever I choose.

To me the most beautiful colors of the day are sunrise and sunset, with their carefully arranged streaks of whites, pinks, violets, oranges, and reds, among the blue skies, everything in between is whatever color you choose in your life. I have gone up and down the river many times, and each sunrise and sunset has been different and unique in its own.

I turned on the starboard engine and then the port engine. At the sound of the engines starting, my body trembled with the fear of not being able to do this. Getting the first three lines untied was pretty easy, but as I started to untie them, I hesitated thinking, "Is this what I really want without him?"

I could hear him saying, "If you don't try, you will never know what you are capable of."

Without thinking twice, I untied the last line; my mind was racing to remember all the things I had helped Brian do. Having that accomplished I put my hand on the throttle and felt his hand guiding mine. Well, his hand must have slipped because I got a little too close to the dock.

Reggie yelled, "I think you may need a little help," as he pushed me away from the dock.

Our boat slip had seemed much wider when Brian was backing out. Checking port, starboard and aft, I continued to back away from the dock.

Reggie commented, "If you go any slower you might as well use an oar. Give it a little more throttle."

I laughed, "Very funny," but it did help ease my tension. Backing out was not as easy as I had hoped it would be. Reggie had to give me another warning.

He yelled, "Watch your port side. You're still too close." The boat on my port side was his, and that was probably why he was so eager to help.

I cleared the dock to my satisfaction and Reggie's approval, taking it out of reverse and putting it into forward, still trembling. I was so engrossed in my fright, at first I didn't hear my friends on the dock cheering and applauding. If they only knew how completely frightened I was.

I checked port and starboard, making sure the entrance to the river was clear. I was on my way. *Why had I been so fearful? That was pretty easy, so far.*

The end of the no wake zone was in sight. Once again doubt and fear had begun to take over. The next step, putting the boat on plane, trimming it for a smooth and efficient ride would be a test of my new skills. Now was the time to remember all I had watched Brian do when he had tried to explain it to me. I wanted to close my eyes and picture him once again, but that was not a wise thing to do. I tried so hard to hear his voice in my head, but I was on my own.

Now remember, you have to go from idle to at least twenty knots, staying in the river channel until you reach, darn, what number buoy was that I had to reach, oh yes, number seven. Why do I have to stay in the channel until then? Oh right, because of the rocks and sand. Have to stay away from them. How many miles to that buoy? I guess it doesn't matter, just look for it. No, remember how far out it is.

While the boat continued to gain speed with each thrust of the throttle, I became aware that my racing heart and brain had begun slowing down to normal.

Brian must have decided I had too many things to remember and needed help. For no reason at all, I glanced at my wedding ring with four diamonds. *Four miles. That's it, four miles to buoy number seven.*

Brian had always taken the boat to that point and when we reached the bay, let me take over. This time he wasn't there. It was all up to me.

I can't and don't want to do this alone. What made me think I wanted this without Brian? Tears began to fill my eyes. All I wanted to do was to turn around and never set foot on that boat again. Then I knew I wasn't alone, Brian was standing next to me. For one brief moment I could see the smile he would have had when I accomplished a feat I thought impossible. I turned to say, "Thanks," suddenly realizing he wasn't there.

Reaching a comfortable speed, the tears became tears of the joy of accomplishment. At the helm, his hand was on mine, guiding me on my way out to the bay. The fear on my face turned into a smile. Buoy number seven was in sight. *I did it; I actually did this alone.* I continued several miles further before cutting the motor and dropping anchor.

The calmness of the water early in the morning gave me a complete sense of tranquillity I had not felt since Brian's death. Out here he was with me, and there was nothing to interfere with my thoughts and memories. That is where I would spend the entire day. I needed to be alone to decide where my life was going.

Looking at the chair Brian had sat in that last morning, I slowly walked up to it, unable to touch it. I sat on the deck next to it. Looking up as if he was still sitting there, I asked, "Brian, why did you have to leave me? Where do I go from here? Please help me make the right choices. I don't know if I want to continue coming back to Michigan in the summer to our boat and friends at the marina without you. Yet, if I give it up, I will be giving up a part of you."

Late afternoon soon approached, and it was time to return. Helen and Reggie had kept in touch with me during the day. A brief radio message said it all. "On my way back. Appreciate any help offered upon return."

With the marina in sight, I could see Reggie waiting at my slip. He hollered, "Would you like me to move my boat and give you a little more room?"

I hollered back, "Don't be silly. Of course not. I have insurance."

I thought that docking should be easier. Boy, was I wrong. It was as difficult for me as leaving. I had to make several attempts before succeeding. Helen and Reggie helped with the lines, reassuring me, "We knew you could do this with no problem."

After a few days, I decided to try this completely alone. After lunch I set out for the bay. Now I was the captain, not the first mate. Fate hadn't given me a choice.

The beautiful summer day brought back so many memories. Out here I could remember, cry, laugh and let all my emotions take over. I needed to hold on to those feelings without interruption. This is where we had spent our last days together and where he promised never to leave me.

I sat for hours reliving in my mind our life together and especially the last days. As we had lain in bed wrapped in each other's arms all night long, we had talked about our future. We had done that many times, but somehow that time seemed different. A chill came over me as if he wasn't there. I held him tighter.

He had smiled, "If you hold me much tighter, I won't be able to breathe."

I reluctantly let him slip out of my arms, still feeling the warmth of his body as he lay next to me. We had fallen asleep holding hands.

During the next few weeks, everything had been pure magic. I couldn't remember a more perfect summer. The days were filled with sunshine; light fluffy white clouds scattered in the blue sky, and extremely calm waters. There had been occasional light rains, but only at night. The days were like a movie set, everything made to be perfect.

Even the nights were more beautiful than ever. We were the closest we had ever been. One particular evening, we had played our favorite songs and danced the night away. He gently pulled me toward him, and I could feel his strong arms around me, as we made gentle love as never before. With each kiss I began to feel as though we were no longer two souls but one.

Those days had been incredible. We stayed in bed longer than usual each day and got less sleep each night. We would wake during the night, make love and hold each other until we would fall asleep again. Each time he touched me, my body seemed to hold on to his touch and would not let go. The warmth of his body seemed to pass through me like a radiant light. I could feel his love flowing through me. I never wanted this to end. Life couldn't have been more beautiful and fulfilled.

We had married right out of college and in three weeks, on the twentieth of July, it would have been our eighth anniversary. I told myself that this was more happiness than anyone should be allowed to have. It almost seemed sinful to be so happy.

It was the weekend and we had plans to join friends for dinner at a restaurant in town, so we came back to the marina earlier than usual, missing the sunset that night.

Early the next morning, when I had wakened, Brian's side of our bed was empty. I got up, went on deck and saw him sitting there just looking out at the sunrise. I called his name and he didn't respond. Thinking he had fallen asleep after rising much earlier than usual, I walked up behind him, put my hands on his shoulders and gave him a kiss on the top of his head. In that moment my world was shattered and all the happiness gone. I remember my screaming out his name as I fell to my knees. Friends were rushing on board. Sirens wailed in the distance and then silence. The next few days were just a blur.

The funeral was private. His ashes were to be thrown across the waters we loved. That is how I became a captain instead of a first mate, traveling the waters in my own private world with the only love I had ever known still by my side. The man that would never leave me was suddenly gone.

"I will never leave you, and I will always be at your side," were the last words he had said to me as we made love for the last time. I remember thinking what a cruel joke life had played on me.

How could I go on without him? I never considered life without Brian. We had made all our plans for the future together. We never mentioned or thought of a life apart. I was surrounded by so many good friends, but so alone. I had left the boat and all the arrangements for its storage up to the manager of the marina and returned home. The following year had been spent trying to put my life back together. Life was unimportant with no meaning or purpose. The days went slowly by as I buried myself in my work. I thought my classroom full of children would be my comfort, but they only reminded me of what would never be. If only we had had a child, I still would have had part of Brian with me.

Now here I was on the boat again, and it was time to decide where my life was going. The sun would be setting soon, and I needed to return to the marina before dark.

Our friends were helping me to hold on to the days we spent together on our boat ironically named, *Forever Together*. They had persuaded me to spend the summer with them and make a decision at the end of the season. Everyone was so supportive.

I tried to continue the life we had shared. I felt so close to Brian when I was out on the bay. Each time I took the boat out, it became easier. If I wanted to leave before dawn to watch a sunrise and return after a sunset, it would mean leaving and returning to the slip in the dark. That would take a little more practice, which I did at night with a lot of help from Reggie. Reggie finally gave me the okay to venture out before dawn and return in the darkness of night, by myself, whenever I felt the need.

Confident that I could handle the boat by myself, one day I got up before dawn to see a sunrise for the first time alone. That particular sunrise held a special surprise for me. It was the glimpse of the top of a lighthouse. The trees, weeds and shrubs had grown so high that it was barely visible. Maybe that was why I had never noticed it before. Suddenly it disappeared. Lost in the wonder of a beautiful sunrise, I forgot about the lighthouse. I expected the colors to be less radiant without Brian by my side, but that didn't happen.

Choking back the tears, I silently murmured, "I know you are here with me, Brian. The beauty hasn't faded. It *is* still here."

I felt the need to be with friends at that moment, so instead of going outbound, I returned to the marina.

The next morning at breakfast I asked Helen, "Do you know anything about that old lighthouse?"

"What lighthouse?"

"The one on the river near the bay."

"You must be mistaken. There isn't any lighthouse there. It is highly unusual for a lighthouse to be on a riverbank. The beautiful colors of the sunrise must have formed a painting in the sky that looked like the top of a lighthouse. The way clouds form images when you stare at them."

Maybe she was right, so I dropped the subject. But I didn't forget what I thought I had seen.

I found myself spending more time on the river looking for the lighthouse, with no further sightings. *Was it real, my imagination, or were the clouds playing with my mind?*

CHAPTER 2

A group of us were once again outbound on the river going out to the bay and on our way to a little village called—what else—Lighthouse. We had been there many times. We browsed through the little shops; there were many pictures and stories about all the lighthouses in the area. For the first time, I started to actually read the histories of them. If one needed or wanted a lighthouse collectable, that was the place to find it. I went off by myself determined to find some information about the one that I had seen. No one else had ever seen it, to my knowledge.

The others were calling me for lunch and I told them I would catch up with them for dinner. I searched for hours, looking at hundreds of pictures and reading all the captions under each one. Nothing turned up.

The trip home was not a pleasant experience. A severe storm had begun to form and the waves were dashing against the boat tossing me around. Suddenly, as swiftly as the storm hit, it calmed down. At that point, the sun was beginning to set, and the clouds started to open up to show a beautiful emerging sky. It looked as if someone had taken a large paintbrush and drawn long red, pink, and white stripes in the brilliant blue sky.

That was like no other storm I had experienced. I looked up at the sky, and the lighthouse came into view. It seemed to be trying to rise above the overgrown bushes and trees to reach the sky and engulf itself in the colors of the sunset. Being a little—no a lot—under the weather from all the tossing, I was too ill to even mention it to the others. They surely would have thought that I needed more psychological help than they could give me. I was beginning to think they were right.

A few days later, while a group of us were sitting on the dock, I mentioned the event. Everyone laughed and asked if I was still seeing lighthouses that didn't exist. I began to question the incident and my own sanity. Maybe it was my mind playing tricks on me.

Our life as boaters had been easy, never being blessed during our eight years of marriage with children. We had no family obligations. Both being in the teaching profession had made it easy to spend all summer on our boat. I had been afraid of the water when we first met, and he had loved it so. He taught me not to fear it, but to respect it and learn from it.

Forgetting about the lighthouse, I set out for a sunset cruise by myself, something I now did quite often. My boat was just the right size, a 340 Waterway, to handle alone. Reggie or one of the other guys always managed to be around to help me dock when I returned.

Brian and I had planned to get a larger boat the year he slipped away from me. Still another unfulfilled dream with so many heartaches to take its place, and so many lonely nights. My boating friends all admired me for not leaving the group and for all that I had accomplished by myself. They were my salvation, and I couldn't lose them too. To them I was a survivor. In reality, I was devastated and covered it well.

The sun was exceptionally bright that evening. That made it difficult to watch the sunset. Suddenly, there it was. I cut the engine and sat there staring at the lighthouse. For some strange reason it kept appearing and disappearing. What was going on? Was I losing my mind? Was it a figment of my imagination? It was impossible to get closer to shore. The water was too shallow. The exact location was programmed in my brain. I would be able to show Helen and Reggie the exact spot now.

The very next day, right after breakfast, Helen, Reggie and I went out to the river in search of the lighthouse. I had them convinced it existed. Unable to find it, I said, "I must have been mistaken about the location. This whole area is all overgrown with weeds and trees and it looks pretty much the same in all directions. I apologize for insisting you come here."

Helen said, "Don't worry about it. It is a perfect day for a boat ride, so all is not lost. Things are very different for you now. I think you have too much on your mind."

Helen could tell by the tone of my voice that I was upset.

"What do you mean? Do you think I am imagining things?"

"No, I'm sure there's an explanation for all of this. Let's go back. We'll try again some other day. If it is there, Reggie and I will help you find it."

By now I was very confused and decided to do a little research at the Register of Deeds Office. To my surprise, there was no evidence that a lighthouse had ever been in that area. I found that there was a small island in that area. I needed a small craft, so I borrowed Reggie's trailer and dinghy. I drove to the launch area, put the dinghy in the water and set out towards the island. It was about a quarter of a mile away from the launch site.

As I got closer to the island, I could see that the trees and brush were so thick that it would be impossible to determine if it was uninhabited. The sky was very overcast that day. Dusk was coming on. I decided to turn the dinghy around and head back to the launch area. Suddenly, magically appearing above the trees, was the lighthouse. *But* why did no one know about it, and why wasn't it recorded? My first thought was that it could have been so old that the records had been lost or anyone who might have known about it was either dead or too old to care. Brian and I had become interested in lighthouses and had planned to look into the possibility of buying one that was no longer in use. We also wanted to visit some of the more popular ones. I never went on with the project. What was the point? He was gone and so was the dream.

I took the dinghy closer to the island, got out and pulled it on shore. The water was surprisingly warm, warmer than I had ever remembered. It was as if there was no water at all, I could barely feel it, and yet my legs were wet up to my knees.

By now the sun was almost gone and night was setting in. The sky was starless, and the moon scarcely visible. Forgetting to take a flashlight, candles, or any source of light was not a smart move. Completely alone, I couldn't understand my calmness. There was no fear. Brian was at my side telling me to trust him and not fear the darkness. Again, as I had done so many times in the past year, I felt his hand leading me through the dense foliage. His touch and the strength of his arms around me had never left, and that must have been what he meant when he said, "I will never leave you." Well, let me tell you now would not be a good time for him to leave. I began to wonder if there were any creatures inhabiting the island and sharing the darkness with me.

Climbing up a slight incline, it dawned on me that I had lost my sense of direction. How was I going to find my way back to the dinghy? The darkness covered me like a blanket. Even if I had remembered to bring a compass—and why would I— without a flashlight, I wouldn't be able to read it. Whenever I had gotten myself into a mess, Brian would laugh and say, "What were you thinking?" I always replied, "Guess I wasn't."

Undoubtedly, coming here alone, was the most ridiculous idea I had ever had. Why hadn't I tried to convince Helen and Reggie to come with me? Brian, Helen, Reggie and I had often explored the 'off the beaten path' beaches when we would go for weekend boating trips.

Off in the distance, I saw something flickering. "Great, now if I only had a jar, I could catch some of those lightning bugs and maybe have a little light," I muttered. But, of course, why would I bring a jar on this little trip? I didn't bring anything else of importance, including my brain. I couldn't believe I was having that conversation with myself. Was it fright? Perhaps.

Carefully walking towards the dim light, I found myself standing right in front of the lighthouse. The light was coming from inside. A small window was covered with dirt that must have been there for at least a hundred years. It seemed to be hiding whatever was inside. I was trying to scrape the dirt away so I could see inside, and I heard, "What are you doing here? What do you want?"

Of course, what does a lady do when in total fright? Right, faint.

When I opened my eyes, I was no longer outside looking in, but inside looking at a small candle and emptiness. At least someone, whoever it might be, had the sense to bring a candle. I was now lying on what appeared to be some sort of cot or small bed.

In a few minutes my eyes became accustomed to the darkness and the faint candlelight. I could see the sparsely filled room. A couch rested against the far wall. It looked very old and faded. In the middle of the room stood a table and two chairs of very plain and simple design. I began to wonder if my host was like the furniture. Once again, where was my fear? The fainting came from sudden fright, not fear. Fear is what my host meant to create. *Boy does this person needs to learn a lot about me.* I tried to determine if I was alone or if my host was nearby. I stood up and walked towards the candle.

Firmly, I said, "Okay, I am here. What now?"

No reply.

"I don't think this game is funny. I'm not playing."

Still no response. Was I alone now? I was certain my host or hostess was gone. Now it was time to panic. I tried the door. It was stuck or locked. It didn't matter. Either way it wouldn't open. The candle flickered. The light was gone. There was total blackness.

With my hands outstretched, trying not to bump into something or someone, I made my way across the room. I knew that there was very little to stumble over. My main goal was to reach the couch, but I couldn't figure out in what direction to go. I could smell the old musty material that seemed to have been sitting in that damp room for ages. I finally reached it. I sat down with the sensation of not being alone anymore. I reached over to see if I could touch someone or something. Nothing. Okay, now I was a little worried. Nothing could be done until morning. Then I would have the daylight to get me out of this. I curled up in a ball and decided to try to sleep.

Thinking sleep was impossible, to my surprise, it came very quickly, and I began to dream. It was so real. I could feel Brian's arms pulling me toward him ever so gently, and the kiss was so real I felt my body wanting him to make love to me. He began to satisfy my every wish. Instantly I sat up startled, alone and crying.

A faint light was coming through the window. It was dawn. The sun was trying to reach the darkness of the room. I could see that there were other windows in the room, but they were also painted with years of weather.

The candle was no longer on the table. There was no sign of one ever having been there. I tried to open a door that obviously led somewhere, but it was locked. Of course, it would be. Why would I expect anything else? I walked over to the outside door and turned the handle expecting to have to use every muscle in my body to open it. It gently swung open. Was I dreaming all of this? No, I didn't think so. Stepping outside, I discovered I had been in a small cottage attached to the lighthouse.

Okay, what is going on here? I decided to just get into the dinghy and go back to the main land and try to figure it out. *Where did I leave the dinghy?* I did a complete search of the island. I couldn't find it. Oh, great, now the dinghy was missing. In my haste to get ashore, I had forgotten to secure it. How do I explain that to Helen and Reggie? Panic time again! Explaining my absence was the least of my worries. My main concern, at that moment, was to find it and get off the island.

This whole ordeal began to concern me. How could I have blindly set out on this search without preparing myself? I was a very structured person and planned every moment of my days. All, that is, except this one.

I made my way through the thick brush to the beach. There, tied to large tree, was the dinghy.

Now that I knew I could get off the island, I decided to return to the cottage. On my way back, I noticed small areas of the land that had been cleared. Maybe the wood was used in a fireplace. In my haste to leave, I hadn't noticed one in the cottage. Confident that I was alone, I walked up to the cottage and tried to open the door. It wouldn't open. Now why didn't that surprise me?

It was late morning and time to get back. I was sure that Helen and Reggie would be concerned. But they wouldn't question me. I must and would return. It would have to be at night because I could not feel the presence of anyone during the daytime. My host left as mysteriously as he had arrived. But did he leave?

A few days passed, and I decided not to mention the island or the lighthouse to Helen and Reggie. I had to go back. The lighthouse seemed to appear only when it wanted to. Why did I see it one day and not the next? Was it really there or was I searching for something in my life that I wanted but couldn't quite reach? Why was my husband so close to me there, closer than ever since his death?

No one needed to know my quest, so I bought a dinghy. Brian and I had ordered one two days before he died. I had cancelled it. I didn't need one. Another dream and another adventure gone. So many dreams for two, only memories for one.

I set out around six p.m., parked the car in the same place as before, put the dinghy into the water and began my adventure. I saw the lighthouse before I reached the island. That was easy. Why was it so difficult the first time? Maybe because I arrived much earlier this time. I went ashore and directly to the cottage.

The door was slightly ajar. Who was there? I pushed the door open and peered inside, almost afraid of whom or what I would see. The room was as I had remembered, except for the candle. The table was bare the morning I had left, and now the candle was back on it. I entered the room and decided to explore. There was a door off to one side that I hadn't noticed before. Of course, it was locked. Was this door the entrance to the lighthouse? It seemed to blend into the wall. A small fireplace in the corner was partly covered with a needlepoint fireplace guard. The floral pattern must have been very colorful when new. It obviously was as old as the furniture. There was a rug under the table. It was so worn, I couldn't decide if the pattern was flowers or overgrown weeds. That room must have been beautiful at one time.

I sat down on the couch. It was a dull solid dark green with an occasional stripe of what might have been white at one time. I took my flashlight and book out of my bag and began to read. The evening turned into total darkness. I found myself unable to stay awake. I didn't know how long I napped, but I woke suddenly. A candle on the table revealed a figure sitting there.

Quietly I said, "Hello."

To my surprise I heard a very soft, "Hi."

Well, that made me feel better. At least he wasn't my imagination.

"I'm sorry to intrude in your home. I presume this is your home."

"Sorta."

"What do you mean 'sorta'?"

"I spend time here when I want to be alone."

"So who does this place belong to?"

"Does it matter?"

"I guess not. Do you live around here?"

"Yes, among other places."

"What kind of answer is that?"

"The only one I have."

"I guess it is none of my business. Is that what you meant?"

"If you say so."

"Do you have a name?"

"Yes. Do you?"

"I asked first. My name is Catherine, and yours is?"

"Why don't you call me 'stranger' since no one knows I'm here."

"Well if this is your retreat, I had better leave." Why did I say that? I really didn't want to go.

Now this guy was really beginning to intrigue me. I got up from the couch and walked towards him. Maybe he would ask me to stay. Maybe he was as lonely as I was and needed company. As I got near the table, I tripped in a crack in the floor and fell forward. He jumped up from the chair and caught me. As he held my arm, a warm feeling came over me.

He quickly let go of my arm and asked, "Are you all right?"

"Yes…just a little embarrassed for being so clumsy."

I looked into his soft blue eyes and saw a smile that made me feel so comfortable. I started to walk to the door and stopped, hoping he would ask me to stay awhile.

"I should go now. I don't want to intrude any longer on your privacy."

"You needn't leave. How long have you been here this time, and can I ask why you came back?"

"I'm not quite sure. Curiosity, maybe."

"Curious about what?"

"You were gone when I woke up the other morning, and I wasn't aware anyone lived here. No one seems to know this place exists. Why?"

"That's a long story." With that, he became very silent. His silence made me feel that he wanted me to leave, but I wanted to stay. Why? This man was a total stranger.

Suddenly he said, "I'll walk you to your dinghy."

I wondered, *How does he know I have a dingy and where I left it? I didn't see him when I arrived.* At the dinghy, he gently held my hand and helped me get aboard, and gave me a firm shove from shore. He started to walk away. Turning his head slightly he asked, "Coming here alone and so unprepared your first visit, what were you thinking?"

Without hesitation I answered, "Guess I wasn't."

Trying to comprehend what had just happened, I put my hand up to my face and covered my eyes momentarily. When I took my hand away, he was gone. *Who is he? Should I go back? Not now, I need time to sort this out.* All the way back to the mainland his touch stayed with me.

That night in bed, trying to sleep, feeling that touch, I tried to remember Brian's, and I couldn't. I asked myself, "Who is that man and why am I still thinking about him? I don't like this at all. None of this makes sense to me." I decided that I would never go back to the island. It wasn't time to forget Brian. I didn't want to. I had found happiness once that was beyond anything I could imagine, and it was taken away. I never wanted to go through that again. My mind said, "Walk away." My heart said, "Stay." I listened to my mind.

During the next few weeks, I began to question my decision. Thank heaven that summer was almost at an end. I would be returning home and going back to teaching for another school year. New York was home.

CHAPTER 3

There was much to be done before the new school year opened and even more when it did. The first month kept me so busy I almost forgot about the island and him. During a meeting in the principal's office I noticed a picture of a lighthouse. All the old feelings came rushing back. I felt the stranger's hand on my arm. I saw his beautiful smile and his eyes looking at me. I shook my head and came back to reality, but it was difficult to concentrate on the meeting.

In my classroom I had all my students to contend with, bringing me back to the real world. First graders can be a handful, but teaching was what I enjoyed. They were so eager to learn, and I had so much to teach them. That didn't leave me much time for fantasizing.

At the same time my social life was filled with dinners, concerts, plays, and small talk with old friends. Boating and the summer were not mentioned. That was my other life.

All too soon, fall with its wonderful colors arrived. Halloween and Thanksgiving took up most of my spare time. Halloween, of course was a big time for my students, and for me since I had resigned myself to doing the planning and decorating myself.

It had been Brian and my tradition to spend Thanksgiving with Ann and Stan. We had been friends since college. Ann was my roommate, and Brian and I had introduced her to Stan. Each Thanksgiving friends and associates were invited to their home for dinner. This year I knew everyone there except one gentleman. He was a few years older than I was, rather good looking with graying temples, which made him even more distinguished. Ann introduced us. He was a corporate consultant. His name was Nick. Working for a very large corporation and traveling much of the time, Ann meets many new people. She's the type of person who makes friends very easily. Ann and I were so much alike in that respect, but lately I had found myself wanting to be alone with my memories.

While we were having after dinner drinks in the living room, I could see that Nick was trying to decide whether to start a conversation with me. Finally, I took the first step, walked over to him and began talking. What was I doing? This was not I! I was friendly, not bold.

Nick was a little shy at first, which made me a little uncertain. I thought perhaps I should politely excuse myself and rejoin my friends, but I really didn't want to. As we continued to keep the conversation going, we began to relax. We had a lot in common. He got up enough courage to ask if I would go to the ballet with him on Saturday. Surprised, I thought, "A date, can I do this? It has only been a year and a half. Would going out this soon make me unfaithful to Brian's memory?"

"Let me think about it. Call me."

"I can do that. I don't want to rush you into anything. Ann told me a little about you. I understand."

Here was someone charming and understanding, so what was I waiting for? Before the evening ended, I gave him my answer. "Yes, Nick. I'd be happy to go to the ballet."

We began seeing each other frequently, depending on his schedule. It was difficult to know when he would be in town. Every date was an experience. We would go to a different restaurant each time and follow it up with a special event. The evenings always ended with a good night kiss. Then Nick would say, "Had a wonderful time. I'll call you very soon."

He began to call much more often than I wanted. This friendship seemed to be taking a turn for which I wasn't quite ready. I enjoyed being with him, and we talked away the hours on each date. But I kept thinking, "How long will he be patient and not expect more than a goodnight kiss?"

I found that I could share most of my thoughts with him and even had the courage to discuss my feelings about losing my husband and the life we had shared. Tears fell as I told him of the promise. That broken promise still left me devastated and angry. Nick's warm, tender smile made it seem as if things weren't quite as bad as I made them out to be.

We had been dating for almost a month when he surprised me with tickets for a new art showing. Of course I was delighted to go. The artist was fairly new, and I hadn't seen any of his works. I asked several friends if they were familiar with him. They had heard that his work was good.

That night at the opening we walked up to the gallery. My heart stopped. The show was called 'Sunset Love'. In front of the building was a large picture of my lighthouse at sunset. Nick saw the look on my face and asked, "Is there something wrong?"

"No, I'm okay."

"If you're ill, we can leave. The showing isn't that important to me. I think the artist might be an old college friend. I wanted to surprise him and have you meet him. We can come back some other time."

"No, I'm all right. I would really like to meet him."

As we entered the gallery, we noticed a sign posted in the lobby. It was an apology from the artist.

"Sorry, I can't be with you tonight. I must be out of town for a few days. Please feel free to ask the gallery personnel to answer questions you may have. I hope you enjoy the paintings."

Nick said, "If he is my old college friend, that would be just like him. Always unpredictable."

As we viewed the paintings, I became very quiet. Nick noticed how interested I was in each one of them. At other showings we had discussed every painting, but this time I couldn't discuss my thoughts with him. Then in a small corner of the room, all by itself, was my lighthouse, exactly as I had seen it many times. Standing next to the lighthouse were a man and woman holding hands, looking into each other's eyes. The painting was titled 'The Promise.' But how did he know? I couldn't remember telling him about Brian's promise to me, but maybe I had.

I wanted to study every stroke of the brush, every detail, every color. I found I couldn't share my thoughts with Nick.

He looked at the painting and said, "Wow! That is undoubtedly the best work I have ever seen him do. He didn't seem to take painting that seriously in college."

I had to meet that artist, or had I already? I was sure that he was my mysterious host from the island. As we walked away, I once again felt the stranger's hand on my arm. The same touch that kept coming back each time I saw a lighthouse or thought of him. Nick knew something was wrong, but, being very kind and sensitive, he didn't pry.

I had never told Nick about the lighthouse and the mysterious man. In fact, I hadn't told anyone. When I returned home last summer, I thought I had left all of that a thousand miles away. Suddenly Michigan wasn't that far from New York. Had I been closer, I would have returned to Michigan as often as possible for the weekends until at least October when the weather would have stopped me from boating. Time and distance were in my favor, or at least I thought they were. I wasn't sure of my feelings, so I never mentioned it. Maybe there wasn't anything to say. I would have to wait seven months before I could find out.

On the way home, we were both exceptionally quiet. There was an air of uneasiness between us. Normally, we would have talked nonstop about each painting and its hidden meanings. What could I have said about the painting of 'my lighthouse'?

Was I the woman in the painting? Who was the man — Brian or the stranger? I needed to find out. Did any of that have anything to do with me? I could only get my answers if I could see the artist myself.

When we reached my apartment, I asked, "Would you like to come in for a drink or coffee?"

"Do you feel up to it?"

"Of course. I really am fine. I was amazed to see how well all those paintings expressed my love for the water."

"Why did you say 'your love'?"

"I meant the love people have for the water, not me personally. Just how well do you know this man? Does he know about us?"

"Why do you ask?"

"Just curious."

"I'm not sure I know him at all, but if he's who I think he is, I haven't seen him in years. He seemed to be a pretty nice guy. I never thought he would become a serious artist. In college he dropped out in his junior year. No one knew why. I talked to a mutual friend who thought because, the artist signs his paintings simply 'Bryant,' that he could be the same person."

We talked about the paintings with a little more ease on my part. I really didn't want to discuss them at all. Maybe I had jumped to the wrong conclusion.

For the first time since we started to date, he asked to spend the night. It was difficult for me to say, "I'm not ready for this." He understood. What he didn't know was that I had been ready until tonight. The whole situation put me back in the cottage with the stranger. Nick thought his rival was the memory of my husband, but in reality he had two rivals, Brian and the stranger.

The dream I had the night I spent in the cottage reoccurred, but this time the man was faceless. It no longer was Brian. The touch wasn't his either. It was the stranger's touch. I knew what I had to do. I had to go back to the gallery and meet the artist whose paintings had shattered my sense of comfort.

The next day after school, I returned to the gallery. The note was still there. I went inside and asked the receptionist, "Is the artist expected to return soon?"

"No, as a matter of fact, he has discontinued his exhibit and will remove the paintings within the next week."

"Why?"

"I don't know. I have been at this gallery for fifteen years, and this has never happened before."

"Did you get to meet him?"

"No. That's another thing I didn't understand. I was never told anything about his personality, so I couldn't write up a bio for a pamphlet about his work. In fact, he refused to have one made."

"Are any of these paintings for sale?"

"No. That's another curious thing. He could have sold every one of them, but he refused to and just pulled the show."

"Do you know where the paintings will be taken after the show?"

"No, he dealt through an agent."

As I thanked her and left, I wondered about the stranger on the island. If this was the same man, where did he do his painting? Certainly not in the room I had been in; but there were other rooms, one was locked. He had to get his inspiration from the island. His paintings were too real, too beautiful to be done in a studio or some dingy room.

It was going to be a long wait until school ended in June. Then I would be on the first plane to Michigan. I would call the dock master at the marina to let him know when I planned to be there. He would take my boat out of storage and launch it for me.

When I wasn't teaching or going out with Nick, I was getting ready for the holiday season. I have always loved Christmas and decorated my apartment as if I had a dozen children to please. I always bought the biggest tree I could find and trimmed it with ornaments I had made over the years and some that had belonged to my mother. Each year I added new ones, from my travels and nautical ones that friends had given me. I guess that's why my trees got bigger over the years. This year, because Nick and I had many friends with small children, we would be doing even more entertaining. The children would really appreciate the Santa decorations and the real Santa Nick had hired.

After the New Year began, Nick convinced me that it was time to find closure with Brian's death and move on with my life. I must admit, he was right. I was very happy being with him and began to think a future together could be possible.

CHAPTER 4

Secrets are not good for a relationship, but I couldn't share my feelings about the lighthouse, the paintings, or the stranger with Nick, maybe because I wasn't sure of what was real or what was fantasy. I began having fears and doubts about returning to Michigan. Nick asked if he could join me in Michigan. He was looking forward to meeting my friends. How could I explain to Nick this driving need to see another man and how important it was for me to go back to find answers that kept me awake at night? I needed to do this alone. Would he understand if I explained why? I would deal with it when the time was right, and time was running out. Only two more weeks left until the end of the school year. I told Nick he could visit, but I needed at least two weeks to get settled. He had no problem with that.

I felt guilty for wanting to be alone that first two weeks, but there were issues I needed to deal with. I asked myself, "Should I forget it and go on with my new life, which is pretty wonderful? Do I dare risk it? Will the stranger be there? Will he want to see me?" In spite of my doubts, I made the trip.

I had hoped for a bright sunny day when I arrived, but it was cloudy with a hint of rain. I decided to take the boat out anyway. According to the weather report, the river and bay would be calm. My main goal was to see the lighthouse. I didn't find it.

I went back to the dock, got the dinghy, and set off for the island. Since it was early afternoon, there was plenty of time before darkness set in. Stepping ashore, I felt a chill, as if I was being watched. There were no signs of life, so I proceeded to walk up to the door of the cottage. I tried to open it but couldn't. The windows were more weathered, making it impossible to see inside. I felt a hand on my shoulder, the touch I couldn't get out of my mind, and then heard his voice, sharper than I recalled, asking,

"Do you want me to open the door for you?"

Frozen in my tracks, I tried to turn around. His tone quickly changed, as he became aware of the effect of his sudden approach.

"I'm sorry. I didn't mean to startle you."

"'Startle' isn't exactly the word I would use. It is more like 'petrify'. Where did you come from?"

"I'm really sorry. I was on the other side of the lighthouse and heard your motor."

My face must have been as white as the shirt I was wearing. I thought, *Oh, no. Please don't faint again.*

"I think you should sit down or I'll have to carry you into the cottage again."

As he extended his hand to help me, I stepped back. Afraid of the influence his touch would have on me, I assured him I was fine. He respected my wishes and backed away.

"It was very rude of me to refuse your help. I apologize, but every time we meet, you seem to have the need to scare me half to death."

"Well, this is my place and I really didn't invite you."

"Now who is being rude? I'm sorry. You're right. I am an uninvited guest."

He took a deep breath and asked, "Can we just start over here?"

"I think that would be a good idea."

"I'm not used to having people around. I didn't know anyone knew this place existed but me."

"Well, you can see it from the river."

"That's not entirely true. You can only see it from the river when the sun is rising or setting. Think about it."

He was right! I had gone up and down the river during the day and never seen it. That explained why no one else had seen it either. There were so many questions running around in my head. Would he answer them if I gained his confidence? Boy, that was really going to be a challenge. From the expression on his face, I could see he knew that I believed him.

"I'm really not trying to intrude on your privacy. I didn't know you would be here."

"Well, I was here when you came by last year. Why would I be gone this year? By the way, I was pretty nice to you then, but you didn't return. Why not?"

"You wanted me to come back?" I asked with astonishment.

"Yes, I did."

"But why?"

"I don't know. Maybe it was your smile, the touch of your hand, your perfume, I don't know. When I found you sleeping on the couch, I knelt down, and you reached over in your sleep and touched my arm. I still feel that touch."

"Why didn't you ask me to come back?"

"I don't know. But I hoped you would return."

"I really had a hard time staying away. Each time I took the boat out, I wanted to stop and see you, but I thought you wanted to be alone. Otherwise you would have asked me to come back some time."

"Why did you leave so abruptly?"

"I'm not sure. Actually, I wanted to stay. I don't know why I didn't. I was dealing with a problem, and it was more than I could handle at that time. I didn't need complications in my life. The fact that I couldn't get you off my mind or forget the way I felt when you touched me, confused me." I couldn't believe I was telling him this.

He asked, "And now how are those complications? Have you come to terms with them?"

"I can't answer that. I don't know. That's why I'm here. I know the attraction is still there."

He walked over to me and held out his hand. I didn't know what to do. I knew what I wanted to do. I couldn't move. He reached over and took my hand. We entered the cottage, and walked across the room to the couch. We sat down. I wanted to ask if he was the artist in New York. There were no visible signs of any art supplies. He asked me a lot of questions about myself, and I seemed to answer without thinking. His voice was like velvet, and I was mesmerized. Each time I asked a question, he answered it with a question, shifting the focus of conversation back to me.

For hours we talked about life, politics, religion, music and whatever other subject came up. At times we laughed until we had tears in our eyes. Sometimes I could read him like a first-grade book, and then at other times his thoughts were veiled and shadowy. One moment he would give me a big smile and then the next moment appear to be miles away in thought, not hearing me at all.

Sometimes I would ask, "You didn't hear me, did you?"

He'd reply, "Yes, I did."

And yet he didn't answer. I got a big smile but no response or reaction.

I couldn't believe we were talking and laughing as if we had known each other all our lives. We talked about our childhood, and the things we had done as teenagers. Surprisingly we were very much alike. He talked about childhood memories of his mother and then stopped. I got the impression that his mother, for some reason, was not in his life as he grew up. When he wanted to end a subject, there was no way I could get any further information.

Evening was fast approaching, so I said, "I need to leave before I wear out my welcome."

"Will you come back?"

"Of course, if you want me to."

"I wouldn't ask if I didn't want to see you again. Can I call you?"

"I'd like that. I'll write my phone number down for you. Would you mind if I called you?"

He hesitated, then wrote down his number and handed it to me without saying a word, but then he smiled and said, "Call anytime you need a friend."

I thanked him for the conversation and nice afternoon. On the walk to my dinghy, I suggested we meet on my turf. He quickly responded that he never left the island, except for supplies, and I was always welcome there. That was certainly a change from our meeting last year.

I left without asking about the paintings and wondered if I had been wrong. The exhibit in New York could have been a coincidence. I assumed that most lighthouses looked pretty much alike, and at this point being with him was all that mattered.

Not wanting to seem eager, I waited a few days before calling. When I did finally muster the courage to call, there was no answer. When I called back an hour later, he did answer. I mentioned that I had called earlier and casually asked where he had gone. Silence. I had already learned enough about him to know that meant, "Don't go there."

I suggested I bring a picnic lunch to share while we continued our talks and he agreed. Since this time I was invited and expected, he was there to greet me. He had spread a blanket on the grass in an area he had obviously cleared recently. Like everything else on the island, the blanket was worn.

This time the conversation was centered on music. We certainly didn't have the same taste there. He liked country and I'm really not a fan. I like light opera, and he, of course, said it was too hard to understand. I asked if he had ever been to New York and seen any Broadway shows or musicals. His answer didn't give me the information I was looking for. "Not my kind of entertainment."

Why didn't that surprise me? The way he answered so quickly made me feel he was not being honest with me. He let me know what he wanted to and nothing more. He was definitely hiding something. Why did I doubt him? I believed he was being honest with all those questions he chose to answer. I started to analyze his answer. It was possible that he had hired an agent to handle all the deals and never intended to go to the opening. But why had he closed the exhibit and refused to sell his work? Had he decided he didn't want the fame or couldn't live with it? Becoming a celebrated artist would change his life completely. Couldn't he handle that? But then, I could have been wrong. Maybe I wanted him to be the artist because it would have given him a name and identity.

Though he was complex at times, he was really a simple, gentle, person. He seemed to ask little from life and enjoyed the one he had made for himself. Was he happy? Perhaps, most of the time. He never complained or wished for more than he had. It was the moments of silence that made me wonder if I had touched on a subject he was trying to forget. I began to choose my subjects and questions with care.

Family was something that was not mentioned in detail. Being an only child, I had little to say on the subject. I would explore that avenue some other day. It was time to leave, and as I stood up, he took my hand and looked deep into my eyes,

"Bye. I had a good time."

"Do you think I could call you by your name now? I must admit that calling you 'the stranger' has been pretty intriguing."

"You're right. Just call me 'Friend'."

I grinned and raised my eyebrows, indicating I would play his little game for a while longer. He returned the gesture and gave me a big hug. I had to admit this little name game was fun in a way. It kept things interesting. We enjoyed being together. With each visit, I found my attraction to him growing.

I thought he was going to bend down and kiss me but he abruptly backed away. Wanting that kiss, I wouldn't have stopped him. I had fantasized about this moment many times during the past year. But it didn't happen. Maybe that was for the best. If he took me in his arms and kissed me, that could end a beautiful friendship or take it to the next level.

Once more I felt I was being unfaithful, but to whom, the memory of Brian or Nick now? Brian was still very much alive to me when I was with this man. Even Nick hadn't made me forget the life that had been so wonderful and now was gone. That was why I couldn't let Nick completely into my life. Yet I wanted this stranger to be an important part of my life. Why him, why now? My special friend made me very happy and I forgot everything except him when we were together. I hadn't sat down with anyone and talked as freely as I did with him since Brian had died. I told him personal things about Brian and me that I still couldn't tell Nick. When my friend and I talked, he listened, giving me his full attention, and he made me laugh. *It is like being with Brian. There I go again, I can't talk about him in the past tense yet.*

My life was really getting complicated. This man intrigued me, and made me feel alive again. I still couldn't understand or put a label on my emotions. Was it love or pure happiness? Then there was Nick. He could give me everything I ever wanted, including children, and he made me happy. Lastly, there was Brian, the man who had first brought out all of these feeling in me. He singly gave me all that the others did together. I remembered the love and pure happiness I experienced with Brian and how, without warning, it was taken away. Maybe happiness had to come in small doses, and no one could be completely happy without paying a high price. Was I asking too much and heading for more heartache? I couldn't take that again.

The next day he called and asked me to come back to the island. I couldn't stay away. He was waiting for me, and when I reached the shore, he helped me out of the dinghy.

"I thought we would take a walk around the island today," he said as he put his arm around my shoulder.

"That sounds good to me."

"Are you ready for an adventure? You never know what wild creature we might meet."

"What do you mean 'creature'?"

"Just kidding. If you have any fears, you will just have to face them."

Those words made me stop in my tracks. Why did he say that? He was standing behind me, and I quickly turned around. For a split second as I heard those words, I could see Brian. I blinked several times as if to clear my vision and he noticed my uneasiness.

"What's wrong?"

"Nothing. I was just… Never mind. It's nothing."

He put his arm around me again, and we walked along the beach. We stopped for a moment, and he put both arms around me as we stood there, holding each other. I felt so safe, as if that was where I belonged. He tenderly kissed me on the forehead. Not exactly what I wanted, but it was a start. We continued walking, and he stopped, bent down, and picked a little white flower.

"This is my favorite flower, and I don't even know the name of it."

"I'm not familiar with it either. It is beautiful."

He placed the flower in my hair, and we strolled on.

When we got back to the lighthouse, we sat under a tree still holding hands. When I finally got up to leave, he made me promise to return the next day. There seemed to be sadness in his voice this time. He seemed uncertain that I would actually return. I couldn't understand why he would feel that way.

The next day I noticed he seemed a little tired, so I suggested, "If you don't feel like company today, I can make this visit short."

"No, I'm fine. I got up at dawn and started clearing away some of the brush on the other side of the island. The heat must have gotten to me. It's such a hot, humid day."

He quickly changed the subject and asked, "Did you notice the swing I made from the tree I cut down last week?"

I had noticed and admired it. He seemed pleased when I said, "Yes, I did. Let's sit there, and you can relax."

He tried very hard to hide his exhaustion, but it was clearly evident. I finally suggested he get out of the heat and sun. Assuring me he would be fine, and making me promise to return the next day, he went inside. I left with an uneasy feeling.

The next day I arrived at the island around noon to find him fully recovered, even a little adventurous based on his next suggestion.

"I'm going to let you take me for a boat ride today."

Surprised I replied, "Really? You trust me?"

"I've watched you, and you handle that dinghy pretty well."

He had a cooler packed with sandwiches and a bottle of wine. The river was as smooth as glass, and the blue sky was filled with white, fluffy clouds. I had gone up and down this river many times, but today it was as if I were seeing it for the first time. Was it because I was so happy? Neither of us wanted the day to end. Occasionally he would lean over and give me a light kiss on the cheek or my forehead.

"Catherine, I can't begin to tell you how much your friendship means to me. I never want to lose that."

I couldn't find the words to express how I felt at that moment. I put my arms around him and gave him a big hug, but I couldn't look into his eyes. I was aware of how suddenly something so beautiful could end, and I wanted to say, "Please don't promise never to leave me."

The two weeks I spent in Michigan before Nick arrived, my friend and I were together almost every day. Most of my visits were limited to several hours, because I didn't want to answer the questions my friends were beginning to ask. How could I explain my frequent disappearances?

Helen was very concerned about my wanting to be alone, but I explained, "Helen, there are things I need to work out by myself."

"We all understand that you need to move on and in your own time."

Nick would be arriving soon. How would I explain Nick's visit to them? Where does he fit into my life? I knew I wanted my friend in my life, but in what role?

CHAPTER 5

The day finally arrived, and I picked Nick up at the airport. I told Nick I hadn't mentioned him to anyone, and maybe it would be best if he stayed at the hotel the first few nights. I promised to tell my friends soon. He agreed and tried to accept and understand why I had chosen not to tell them when I arrived. Spending time with friends in town was the excuse I used for being gone for a couple of days.

I couldn't bring myself to share with Nick the bed in the cabin of the boat that I had shared with Brian. But sharing my bed didn't seem so bad when I thought of my friend on the island.

Finally I couldn't do this to Nick any longer. I invited everyone to dinner on the third night of his visit. I introduced Nick to them as the new man in my life. They were very surprised and happy, wishing us the best and giving their approval. I needed this blessing from the people who had helped me through the darkest days of my life.

I had to call my friend and explain that I couldn't visit the island for the next two weeks, because I had company from New York. I had to find the words to tell him about Nick, leaving out that we were involved. He was very silent at first and said it was no problem. He made me feel he really didn't care one way or another and I didn't need to explain anything to him. I began to wonder if he cared for me at all, or was I just someone to fill his lonely days? No, that wasn't it. I could tell there was something there, even though all he had done was to hold my hand tightly and look deep into my eyes. I wanted him to take me in his arms and kiss me with as much passion as I knew I could return the kiss. But this was not a reality yet.

As these longings became increasingly stronger, I knew that I couldn't tell Nick anything about the lighthouse or show it to him. I was sure he would remember the paintings, and the questions would start. I would have to tell him what this man meant to me and where he fit in my life. Nick sensed something was wrong, but he didn't pry.

I took him for rides on the river and out to the bay. The weather was beautiful, and the water was like glass. Everything seemed to work out perfectly for us. One night we anchored out on the bay to watch the sunset and decided to spend the night there. I knew Nick expected to share my bed. Was I ready? I decided it was time to find out.

As I lay next to him, I could feel the comfort of his arms, but something was missing. My mind was somewhere else. Why was I pushing him away? Nick was loving, caring, and knew what he wanted and where he was going. I apologized to Nick for my coolness and explained that the boat was the last place Brian and I had made love before he died. He understood and hoped that he could fill that void and ease the memory, replacing it with happier ones.

The next day, on the pretense of personal business in town, I asked Nick if he would like to visit with Reggie while I was gone. Reggie and the other guys liked Nick and suggested a fishing expedition. Nick was not a fisherman, nor did he have any knowledge of the waters and boating. The guys were all in agreement that when they were through with Nick, he would be a changed man.

I left the boat and called my friend. When he answered the phone, he was very astonished.

"Did your friend go home already?"

"No, but I need to see you."

"Why? Is something wrong?"

"Well, no not with my guest. With me."

"I don't understand."

"I need to see you and be with you, and I can't explain it."

"I think you had better go back to your guest, and we will wait until he is gone to talk about it."

"I don't want to wait. It will be another week."

"I need time also, and these two weeks are what we need. I have a lot to do around here. I have big plans for the lighthouse and island, and that will take a lot of time and work on my part."

It struck me strange that he would do this because after the first two visits when I was in the cottage, he never invited me in again. I hadn't found out what was behind the door. I thought it was more living quarters. Perhaps it was where he did his painting. Was he even the artist who I thought he was?

I agreed to stay away until Nick left. Maybe I really needed to give Nick my full attention. The two weeks flew by. We had more fun with my friends than I had imagined we would. He fit in very nicely, and they were right — they made a new man out of him. He really did enjoy boating and fishing.

The girls and I took turns making dinner each night and tried to see who could make the best gourmet meal. One of the girls had spent two weeks in Europe and came back with some really good French entrees. We got into the whole French atmosphere, right down to the language, which no one understood except for a few words. No one except the girl who had been to Europe and Nick, of course. Nick had been to France on business many times. So the two French experts entertained us all evening with their stories about their adventures in Paris, which they weakly attempted to tell us in French. Luckily for us they spoke English with just a few French words thrown in for effect.

With only two days left, Nick asked if he could return soon. He still had a lot of vacation time coming and wanted to spend it with my friends and me. He really did fit in. It seemed that he had taken over Brian's place with the group. They all adored him, and he was so eager to learn all we could teach him about the life of a boater.

By now the island, the lighthouse and my friend seemed to be fading from my memory. I had made up my mind that I would not call him when Nick left, and that whatever there was between us was over. It was apparent I was the one who wanted something to come from this friendship and he didn't, so I didn't need to make a choice. Nick wanted a relationship and me. He fit into my world perfectly.

I didn't know if my friend remembered when Nick was leaving. On the way back from the airport, my mind was on Nick, already anticipating his next visit, when the sound of my cell phone jolted my thoughts.

"I missed you, and I want to see you," were my friend's first words.

Much to my amazement, I said that I was busy and couldn't visit for several days.

I was certain that I was over him, and that I didn't feel the same way since Nick's visit. I had no intentions of returning his call or visiting him again. The touch that had stayed with me for a year without even seeing him or being with him was gone. I tried to imagine it but couldn't. This was a good thing. Now I could concentrate on Nick and our relationship.

My friend called several times each day for the next two days. Finally, on the third day, he called to tell me he was in town and wanted me to meet him for coffee. Coming to town was totally out of character for him. My mind was made up. Nothing was going to change it, but I owed him the truth about Nick and me.

I walked into the coffee shop. He was sitting at a table staring into space. He didn't see me at first. I walked up behind him, startling him. When he turned around, I could see he had a troubled look on his face.

When I inquired about what was wrong, he said, "Nothing. Everything's fine."

I knew him well enough to know that wasn't true. For some reason it didn't matter any longer. If he didn't want to share all his problems with me, I would let him have his privacy. I couldn't find the words to tell him that I couldn't see him anymore. After one cup of coffee, I had to leave. My will was weakening.

"Sorry. I can't stay longer. I really have lots of errands to run."

"I understand. Having company for two weeks, regular routines get interrupted."

"I'm sorry you came to town for such a short time. I hope I didn't inconvenience you."

"Don't worry about it. You didn't. Seeing you made it all worth while. Why don't you come to the island tomorrow? I've missed you so much."

I wanted to hear those words weeks ago but not now. It was too late.

The next day, he called and asked if I could meet him in the park around seven o'clock that evening instead of on the island. I had never known him to come ashore, except for supplies, and now he was coming two days in a row. I don't know why, but I agreed.

As I neared the park, I started to regret my decision. Walking up to the center of the park, I got caught up in all the beautiful flowers along the path. The sun was shining on them, creating the illusion of diamonds and precious gems being held up by their stately emerald green stems, swaying in the gentle breeze. I looked up. There he was, standing in the pathway, his arms reaching out to hold me. It was so natural to just walk into his embrace.

Once again we talked, but the wonderful smile and laughter were gone. I began to worry that something was very wrong with him. I wanted to ask if he was feeling okay, but I knew he wouldn't tell me anyway. He gently took my hand, pulled me towards him, slowly put his hand under my chin, and kissed me the way I had wanted for so long. All the memories and emotions I had worked so hard to forget were back.

There was no doubt in my mind that I had been fooling myself. Nothing had changed. As his kisses became more passionate, I finally knew he felt the same as I. We held each other, and neither said a word. Words were not needed. The only thing that mattered was that we shared the same magnetism. Time was standing still, and I didn't want this moment to end.

Reality set in, and suddenly I was thinking about what I was doing to Nick. As much as I wanted this, I knew that my friend and I needed to talk, and this was not the time. I didn't want to hurt either of them. I was certain of Nick's love. I drew away from the embrace.

A little startled, he questioned my reason, "What's the matter? I thought this was what you wanted."

"I did too, but…"

"But what?"

"I'm sorry. I can't explain it right now."

"What is there to explain? You don't need to explain or apologize. There is nothing to apologize for. It's time for me to leave anyway. I'll be in touch, if you want."

"But you just got here."

"I know, but obviously this is not the right time for what just happened."

How could I let him walk away again? I knew I needed to let this relationship run its course and decide where things were going. I knew so much, yet very little about this person. He was so private and not willing to let anyone into his life except me. Why? He liked to be alone, or at least I thought he was alone most of the time on the island. Again, that was something that I wasn't certain about. I looked into his eyes catching a glimpse of a slight tear, but it was quickly gone. He turned and started to walk away.

"Please don't do that."

"What am I doing?"

"Walking away without even asking for an explanation. I have hurt you."

"No you didn't. I'm all right. Do you want me to call you?"

"Yes, I do."

With that he turned and walked away into the night. With tears in my eyes, I wanted to run after him and ask where we were headed. Why couldn't I express my thoughts when I was with him? I was always at a loss for words when it came to asking about our relationship. Maybe it's because I was afraid of the answers. I sat down on a bench and cried. I finally pulled myself together and slowly walked back to the boat. I waited until he had time to get back to the island, picked up the phone, and called him. The phone rang once, and he answered.

I said, "I'm sorry to call so late, but I really needed to talk to you."

"We did talk tonight."

"No, not about what needed to be said."

"What do you mean by that?"

"We both wanted what happened, and maybe more. You can't deny that."

"Then why did you turn away?"

"There is so much I don't know about you, and I'm not sure where this relationship is going."

"And you do know where your relationship is going with your friend from New York?"

"I made no definite commitments there."

"I told you I don't like commitments. I need to do what I want when I want. I've done that for so long that I can't change now. Maybe someday I'll regret that. Time will tell. You have made me think about the direction my life is taking and whether I need changes. I'm going out of town for a few days. I'll call you when I get back."

It was useless to pursue the conversation further, so we said goodnight and hung up.

These roller coaster feelings were tearing me apart. One day I was up and the next day down. When I was sure things would work out for us, he did or said something that changed my mind. He never admitted he had strong feelings for me. It was something I could sense at times but not always. Was it something I wanted and he didn't? I wanted answers he wouldn't give me, so I decided to do something about it. I also needed to see if he was the artist whose paintings Nick and I had seen.

Since he was going to be gone for a few days, I decided to go to the island and look around for myself. I didn't know how I was going to get into the cottage, but I was willing to try. Knowing how old the cottage must be, I was hoping that any old fashioned skeleton key would work.

The next day I called, and there was no answer. I called several times and still no answer. I decided it must be safe to go.

Nearing the island, I carefully scanned the shore looking for any signs of life. It looked deserted. I was ready to go ashore when two figures appeared. It was he and a woman. They were coming out of the cottage. They were laughing and talking, and then he took her in his arms and kissed her as he had done with me. My heart sunk. Who was she and why hadn't he told me about her? Why did he lie to me and say he was going out of town? My first reaction was shock. Then shock turned to anger. How could I have been so fooled? I could handle the truth but not a lie. After all, I was involved with Nick, and my friend and I never committed to each other. If he was involved with someone, I could understand that, but why lie? Well, come to think about it, he had never lied about anyone else in his life. He simply never had mentioned it.

I had begun to cry when I had first seen the two of them, but as I turned the boat around to leave, those tears were gone. I didn't know if I was numb from the pain or if I had had enough. I couldn't cry. If he called me upon his 'so called return,' should I mention what I had seen and what my quest was that day, or wait for him to explain? I was too angry and I didn't want to hear his lies. Knowing the hold he always had on me, I'd probably believe whatever he had to say. Like I said, "No one deserves so much happiness at one time. Something will always come along and destroy it." I should have learned my lesson. Maybe that is why I couldn't completely commit to Nick. Somehow that would be destroyed also.

On the way back to the marina, I realized that I wouldn't feel all this pain if I didn't truly love him. Why hadn't I seen that this man could give me the love I had lost when Brian died?

When I got back to the marina, I had to keep busy for fear I would change my mind again. All he had to do was tell me the truth. If he lied about this, how could I ever trust him again? How much of our friendship was a lie? Was that woman his secret?

CHAPTER 6

It had been a week and no word from him. Was this how he was going to end the friendship before it became a relationship? Nick was coming today for another visit. I didn't have time to think about anything else. I went to town to do some grocery shopping and pick up a bottle of champagne to celebrate. I was ready to tell Nick I could make a commitment.

I took my time picking out two perfect steaks, portabella mushrooms, and the makings for a Caesar salad. I wanted everything to be perfect his first evening back. Mae, the checkout girl, remarked that someone was going to have a very special night. I smiled, giving her the distinct impression that I certainly hoped so.

At a quick pace, almost running to the car, I continued to think about Nick's arrival in a few hours, and needed to get home to get myself ready. I wanted to look special for him. My only thoughts were of Nick. My friend and all my unanswered questions would remain that way and the door to that part of my life would stay closed forever.

Hearing my cell phone ringing, I quickly opened the car door. Before I got in, I answered it, hoping Nick wasn't going to be late. I really did want to see him. The voice on the other end was not Nick.

"Hi. How are you? I've missed you while I was gone. I would like to see you."

My heart stopped. I was not ready to talk to him. The one thing that always had gotten to me was his voice. It was so soft, low, and sexy. I could picture his wonderful smile every time he spoke. A smile that made me forget, at that moment, everything except being with him.

"I'm fine. Your trip took longer than you planned."

"Other things came up that I wasn't planning on."

"Really? And what would that be?"

"I don't think you would be interested. It was just business."

"You don't know what I would be interested in because you really don't know me, and I don't know you."

"What does that mean?"

"I can't explain that now. I have plans for tonight and have to go."

"I'm sorry I interrupted you. I'll call you tomorrow. We really do need to talk. I'll explain everything."

Determined that this goodbye would be our last, I had no intention of listening to his lies. I'd screen my calls and not answer. Someday, before I left for New York at the end of vacation, I'd let him know what I had seen and that Nick was going to be the main person in my life now. I needed a stable relationship. I could forgive anything but a lie. The truth might not have been what I wanted to hear, but it would be better than a lie.

Faltering, unable to find my car keys, I glanced across the street, and there he was looking at me with his phone still in his hand. I turned around and the tears were starting. I didn't want him to see what he had done to me. He quickly crossed the street towards me. He took my hand. Finding my keys, I pulled away and got in the car, not looking back. I was afraid that if I saw any look of remorse on his face, I would probably fall into his arms. All I ever wanted was to understand him and to have a commitment on his part.

Once again I walked away from the man I really loved, certain he didn't love me, because he had only shown me deep friendship, not love. I was unwilling to put myself in that situation again. My plans with Nick had been made. Loving Nick, I would some day be *in* love with him. Glancing into the rear view mirror, I could see him standing there, confused, watching me drive away. How was I going to get through this night now, a night so wonderfully planned?

As if he knew what I needed, when I got back to the boat, Nick was waiting there. He had been able to catch an earlier flight and wanted to surprise me. Reggie and Helen had picked him up at the airport. I had had enough surprises for one day. Now it was going to be my turn to surprise Nick with what he had been waiting to hear for such a long time. Yes, it had been too long in coming and now was the perfect time. They say, 'timing is everything.'

Nick and Reggie decided to take a short boat ride on Reggie's new jet boat. That was okay with me because there was a lot to do before dinner. I quickly began preparing the things that could be done ahead of time.

Helen offered to set the table and get out my good linen, china, and candles so I could get ready. The meeting in town didn't spoil my plans. Eagerly, I started to get dressed, rehearsing how I would tell Nick that we had a future together.

Everything was set. Helen wanted to prepare the dinner, serve us, and leave. We both believed it was a good plan and were like two schoolgirls talking about my date.

Nick arrived from his boat ride around six, and dinner was ready. He laughed when he saw what Helen and I had planned. Reggie also wanted to be part of this little plan and decided to be our waiter and serve the wine. Dinner was served, and our waitress and waiter disappeared.

After dinner, I took Nick's hand as we walked from the boat down a path into the park. Reaching the center of the park by the water fountain, I stopped and turned to him. He took me in his arms and, after a very passionate kiss, held me tightly. All at once I remembered holding my husband that tightly before he slipped away from me that last night. Fear began to take over, and I didn't know if I could tell Nick what I had planned. Would this dream also end? Would this happiness be taken away? I began to tremble, and he held me tighter.

"What's the matter? Are you cold?"

"No, I was just thinking how I would feel if I ever lost you."

"Why would you think that? I would never leave you? If you walked away from me, I'd run after you. I will never let you go. I love you too much."

I remembered how I had just walked away from my friend. He didn't try to stop me. My fears about Nick lifted like a heavy cloud that had been encircling me. The words 'There is nothing to fear;

just learn from what you fear and respect it' came back to me.

No one had ever told me how you could love two men equally and how to decide which one was right for you. It isn't something you read in a book. I was at that point in my life right now. All I could do was hope and pray I had been right.

Taking a deep breath, I started, "Nick, you surprised me with your early arrival today, and now it's my turn to surprise you. I've been thinking."

"Really? What about?"

"I'm ready to plan a future with you."

He looked at me with so much love. "I have waited to hear those words and had begun to think I never would."

His eyes filled with tears of joy. I knew I hadn't made a mistake. That night became the best night we had spent together. Even making love was perfect. We started to make plans for our future. After Nick had fallen asleep, I lay awake thinking. My mind began to wander. Not having made love with the other man in my life, it was easier for me to make the right choice. 'You never miss what you never had' is an old saying but, in the back of my mind, I still wondered what it would have been like.

Since no one knew about my secret love, I would keep that secret and memory locked in my heart forever. I felt safe in assuming he would never talk about us to anyone. If he had friends, he never mentioned them. There was no need to tell Nick. In reality nothing had developed between us except a strange bond of friendship. He once told me that he would always be my friend, and maybe that was all he really did want. I truly did love him, and I had to walk away. I realized that this was the hardest decision I had ever had to make in my life. It was a love that could never be and a life that would never be. How could I love someone so much and give it all up? I think he felt the same but for some reason couldn't admit it to himself or me. I wish I had been able to open the doors of his life that he kept closed and refused to open. What was he hiding from that was too painful to face even with the love and support I would have given him? Who was that woman?

I knew I would not be able to sleep, so I got up and sat on deck trying to sort out my thoughts and emotions. I remembered the first time I had seen my friend. If someone had told me it was possible to love at first sight, I would have seriously questioned it. I had found out it was true. From the very beginning, I had known he was someone I needed and wanted in my life, not even knowing who he was or his name. I didn't realize how much until I gave him up. I would always feel his touch, see his bright smile, and remember his soft voice. That was something I couldn't share with anyone. Nick must never know. If I told him, it would destroy our chance for happiness. Knowing all this, I had to see him once more and tell him about my commitment to Nick.

The next morning Nick and I invited all our friends to the local café and told them about our impending engagement. Everyone was so pleased and wanted only our happiness and a full life for us. Nick wanted to be married within the next few months, but I convinced him there was no rush. We wanted everything to be perfect with all our friends from the marina and New York present. I had plenty of time for arrangements. I wasn't going to return to teaching for at least two years. I had all fall, winter, and spring to plan my wedding.

CHAPTER 7

Nick's week was up, and he had to return to New York. I had another week before putting the boat in storage and returning home. After dropping Nick off, I dreaded the next stop — the island. My heart would break, telling him my plans, mainly because I knew it wouldn't devastate him as it did me. That part of my life was ending.

I got in the dinghy and set out for the island. The tears were flowing so hard I wanted to turn back, but I had to end this. Seeing him, would I be able to find the words I had gone there to say? I turned the dinghy around and went back to the marina. I sat down and wrote a letter.

The day before leaving for home, I set out with the hope of not seeing him. As I approached the island, I could see that his boat was gone. I walked up to the cottage and slid the letter under the door. My life would never be the same, and I would always wonder how it might have been. I wanted to see his reaction as he read the letter, but that couldn't be, so I simply left. I should have delivered the letter the day I was to leave, but I guess I was still hoping for some sort of response or emotion. It read:

My dearest friend,

By the time you read this, I will be preparing to return to New York. I needed to let you know that Nick and I are planning to be married in the near future. First, I must tell you how I have always felt even though I couldn't say the words when we were together. I don't know how you felt about us or even if there was an 'us'. I loved you from the first moment I saw you. I know it sounds crazy, but it's true. I realize that now. I still see you sitting next to me, and the way you would look at me. At that moment I thought, "This is the man I want in my life." I didn't know your name, if you were married or single, or anything about you. I couldn't explain my feelings. As our friendship grew, I kept fighting the fact that it was love. The times we spent together made me happy and alive again. I never thought I could be happy or love again, but I did. There were times I thought you felt the same, but you would back away. The next moment I felt you didn't care at all. I was never really sure about your feelings. I wanted more than you were willing to give, but I couldn't break through whatever was stopping you from loving or caring about me. I tried so very hard to let you know how I felt, but the words wouldn't come. So now I need to let you know before I walk away again. The first time I left you was a big mistake, but this time it is necessary. I love you too much to just be your friend. I know you can't return that love. I also need to let you know that when you told me you were going out of town, I went to the island and saw you with a woman. Why I was there is not important. I saw you kiss her, with the passion you couldn't show me, and I couldn't bear it. I only hope now that she is part of your life and you will be happy. I wanted so desperately to make love to you, but you never once suggested it. I know that you don't share this love I have for you, so I need to go on with my life realizing I'm capable of loving again. I thought that I loved you enough for the both of us, and you would someday return my love. Part of me will always love you and never forget you. Knowing you has made me a stronger person. I will always be grateful for those times I couldn't bear the loneliness and anger of losing Brian, and you would take my hands and hold on so tight telling me I would get through it because I was strong and a survivor. When you have dark moments, always know that I'm out there somewhere, loving you and wishing all the best for you. Maybe someday you will be able to love as I have loved you and to feel my presence as I will always feel yours. I will never forget or stop loving you.

Friends Forever.

I waited for the phone to ring or for him to come to the boat. I wanted him to take me in his arms and tell me that he had always loved me also. I wanted him to make love to me as I had imagined it could be. That was the longest night of my life with no resolutions. The next morning I reached for the phone every five minutes to call him. But I couldn't dial the number. I didn't want to hear the rejection I would once again get, —'friends forever, lovers never.'

As I waited at the airport, hoping he would stop me from getting on the plane, I finally resigned myself to the fact that it would never happen. I boarded the plane and knew my life was now starting over, and he would never be part of it again. As the plane started down the runway, I sat back with just my thoughts and memories.

On the trip home, I tried to make myself believe I had done the right thing, but I couldn't. Our lives were so different. I knew so much, yet so little about his life, and my love wasn't enough for him.

I still didn't know if he had been the artist in New York. All Nick had to say was they called him 'Bryant' in college. I really didn't know his full or real name. We parted as Catherine and 'Friend.'

I wanted a home, children, and someone who would always be there without secrets. Ironically, I was starting my new life with a secret that could destroy what Nick and I had built. After all, it was only a deep friendship. If Nick accepted this and still loved me and wanted me, nothing could come between us. If he couldn't, I would lose him. I had already lost two men I loved very much, and I couldn't bear to lose Nick as well.

My life was so complicated now. Not at all like my first love. Brian and I had met in high school and went to college together. We had been so much in love, and were married right after college. It wasn't love at first sight but a love that had blossomed, as we grew as a couple. When we had decided to buy a boat, neither of us had actually known anything about boating. It was something the both of us would master. Our life together had always been sharing and learning together.

When we learned that Brian could never father a child, we worked through it together. All our plans, thoughts, and dreams were as if we were one. We were truly soul mates. I kept asking myself, "How could I have fallen in love at first sight with a perfect stranger?" My friend was nothing like Brian. There was no comparison. Yet when I compared Brian and Nick, I saw the same qualities in Nick, as I had in Brian.

The plane arrived on time, and Nick was waiting at the gate for me. Seeing him with all the love in his eyes and his happy smiling face, I knew my secret would always have to remain a secret. Right or wrong, that decision had to stand if we were to have a future together. I had to justify my decisions for myself. My friendship with my friend had been right, telling Nick would be wrong.

When we got into the car, Nick casually remarked that he had to make a stop before we reached my apartment. He stopped by a floral shop. He came out carrying a single red rose, opened my car door, and handed it to me with a kiss.

It was good to be home. Nick opened the door to my apartment, and the living room had been filled with dozens of red roses. As I was putting the single rose in a bud vase, I noticed a small envelope attached to the red bow. I opened it, and inside was the most beautiful marquee cut diamond ring I had ever seen. With tears in his eyes, Nick slipped the ring on my finger and asked, "Are you ready to be my wife?"

"Yes," wasn't hard to say even through my tears of joy.

The next day we called Ann and Stan and invited them to dinner the following evening. We thought that Ann and Stan should be the first to know the wedding date — the first day of June — since they had been responsible for our meeting. They were very pleased. Stan insisted on giving the bride away. Ann had a million plans for the wedding, and I asked her to be my matron of honor.

Ann said, "Well, Michigan must be the magic place."

Her remark took me by surprise, and I asked, "What do you mean?"

"That's where the two of you decided you belong together."

Nick was beaming and replied, "It certainly is."

Just hearing the word 'Michigan,' I suddenly had the urge to share my secret with someone. Ann had always been my best friend, and we had always told each other everything, well almost everything. Ann noticed a slight tear.

"Why the tears?"

"They're tears of joy." Would his memory and my love for him haunt me forever?

CHAPTER 8

As the days became weeks and the weeks flowed into months, things got much better. My 'friend's' smile and that low, soft voice faded again. Apparently time and distance accomplished that. I didn't want to return to Michigan. I suggested to Nick that we sell the boat and start an entire new life. My decision was a complete shock to Nick. All I had to do was hear his voice and it would all begin again. Maybe this time it would be different, but I didn't want to take the chance of finding out. I had gone through this before.

Totally shocked, Nick said, "Sell the boat! But why? We love it, and what about all of your friends that helped you through such a difficult time in your life? If you think you are doing this for me, you're wrong. You made me love your life, and it is part of our life now."

"I just thought that when we decide to start a family, it might be difficult to continue that way of life for an entire summer."

"I'm sure our children will learn to love it as much as we do. Remember I had never been on a boat until I met you. And look at what you and your friends have done for me. But if this is really what you want, then sell the boat. I want whatever makes you happy. Think about it before you make a final decision."

"I will," I said, knowing that there was nothing to think about. Reconsidering was impossible.

I wished so much it would have been possible to tell Nick the real reason I wanted to sell the boat. By selling, I wouldn't have to return to Michigan or 'him'. That was the only solution. I would always want to see him if I would return, and that could never be now. I had made up my mind and would abide by it.

Ann and Stan were wonderful. Ann planned an engagement party for us with all our close friends invited. The decorations were absolutely perfect. On the table were little boats filled with candy and nuts. The placecards were outlined with pictures of little school supplies, and the napkins were printed with computers, phones, and brief cases. She covered all of the bases for us.

It was nice seeing my fellow teachers again since I hadn't returned to the classroom that year. I really had missed working each day, but there was so much to do and so many plans to make. We had already agreed that I wouldn't return to work after we were married since we wanted to start a family as soon as possible. The idea of being a mom scared me a little, even though it had been my dream for many years. Now I could be one of those moms helping the teacher instead of being the teacher trying to get the moms to help.

A garden wedding in June would have been perfect at Ann and Stan's, but Nick wanted to be married in church. He agreed to the garden for the reception. Since I had gone through this before, I decided to let Nick plan that part of the wedding.

Ann and I went shopping for the perfect dress. I wanted something that would be appropriate for a second wedding. We decided on ivory, not white. At a small boutique I found what I had been looking for. The gown was sleeveless. It was made of ivory lace with a v-shaped neckline. The bodice had satin red roses with stems and leaves made of tiny pearls. The a-line skirt flowed to my ankles. The sales lady showed us a wide brim lace hat with the same roses. Ann felt as if she was planning the wedding of the sister she never had.

I tried to keep my mind on all the arrangements, but I found myself thinking about him and wondering what he would be doing. I had to convince Nick to either sell the boat or move it closer to New York. But we loved Michigan. If I told Nick the truth, I was sure he would understand and not return. I felt it was the only solution. When Nick came home from work, I told him we needed to talk.

"Oh boy. When someone says 'we need to talk' that usually means there is a problem. I told you that the wedding plans are all yours. Whatever you want is what I want, but tell me, what's the big problem? Is it what color flowers or napkins I would like?" he said with a chuckle. "Seriously, what do you need?"

I looked into his loving eyes and couldn't say anything. I sighed, "Oh, never mind, it wasn't anything. I'm just a little nervous with so many plans to make."

"Come here." He gently took me into his arms and kissed me. How could I break his heart and give this up? I couldn't.

The invitations were sent out and the responses began coming in. Our friends from the marina were all coming. Ann and Stan had a very large house with three guestrooms and had offered them to our Michigan guests. A few of the girls I had worked with at school also offered their spare rooms. We wanted everything to be perfect for all our friends who would come to share in this wonderful event.

The day finally arrived. Ann and Stan drove me to St. Albin's Church. Stan walked me down the aisle, and when I saw Nick waiting for me at the alter, I wondered, "How could I have doubted my love for him and even thought of giving him up for a one sided love?"

Nick and I said our vows together. "I promise to love you always. I will be there for you in any situation or problem. We will face life together through happiness and sorrow."

Holding hands, Nick and I repeated our vows together, and the only touch and kiss I felt was Nick's. I truly believed nothing could ever come between us.

We had our garden reception at Ann and Stan's, and everything was flawless, from the beautiful flower gardens to the cloudless blue sky. June was the perfect time for a wedding. I found pure happiness again and wasn't afraid of losing it. It was very clear to me now that my secret love was sent to teach me how to find happiness and love again, even though it wasn't with him. He was my teacher, not my lover. I finally said good-bye.

We took a two-week honeymoon to Hawaii. Walking along the beach in Maui, my only thoughts were of my husband. As we walked hand in hand, I had a quick flash of 'him' as he always held my hand, but it quickly left as Nick turned to me and gently kissed me.

"You've made my life complete. I will always love you. You will never be unhappy. I'll see to that. I want to start a family as soon as possible. What do you think of that?"

"All I ever wanted out of life was to be the best wife and mother possible. I will spend the rest of my life doing just that for you."

Nick could take care of us very comfortably, and I would never have to return to work. The only teaching I wanted to do was to my own children.

The sunrises and sunsets were as beautiful as we had ever seen and the colors of the days were exactly what we chose to make them. They were as bright as all the flowers, blue skies, and fluffy white clouds. As the winds created slight breezes, you could smell the sweet aroma of all the flowers, something the rarest perfume couldn't capture or duplicate. We didn't want this to end, but we knew it would and we vowed to return. We changed our departure time and took the red eye home because we wanted to see one more sunset before leaving. We had dinner in our room overlooking the ocean and watched the sunset.

I silently whispered a thank you to my special friend and teacher. I knew that I would never forget him and would always hold him in a part of my heart. At times, I wondered if he was really there or just the ghost of Brian trying to help me live again.

I was so sure that all my feelings for my friend were gone. I rarely thought of him and could look at a picture of a lighthouse and see just that, nothing more. There were no more memories of the days and evenings I had spent with him.

While we had been on our honeymoon, the dock master had called and had left a message. He wanted to know if we would be using our slip or if he should sell it for us. Nick said, "You've had time to think about this. What should I tell him? If we sell the slip, that means we sell the boat too. I need to call him back. What do you want to do?"

"What do you want to do?"

"No, that's up to you. I have a lot of good memories, and I'm sure you do too. You'll have to decide if the good ones outweigh the bad ones. I'll do whatever you want."

I decided that Nick was right. I said, "Call the dock master back and tell him to launch our boat."

CHAPTER 9

Two days later, we had arranged for the dock master to put our boat in the water. Nick wanted to sell the boat and get a larger one, but we decided to wait until the next year. We wanted to take our time and get something big enough for our future family. We were also working on that.

Nick needed to return to work, so I went to Michigan myself. Sitting on the plane, I thought about all our friends and looked forward to a wonderful summer. Nick decided to lighten his workload and later spend the rest of the summer at the boat. Thanks to the computer, a lot of his work could be done from the boat. He wouldn't take any new clients until the end of summer.

Helen and Reggie met me at the airport, and it was non-stop talking between Helen and me. Reggie just rolled his eyes and voiced his opinion that it was a good thing we weren't parted any longer.

It was one of the hottest mid-July days that we could remember. Reggie had the boat ready and was taking us out for a ride. We would anchor out on the bay, have dinner and watch the sunset. It sounded like a great plan to me! I began missing Nick terribly and wanting him to be with me.

After unpacking and checking out the boat, I sat on deck for a few minutes. Memories of last summer with Nick and the time we spent on the boat brought a smile to my face. This summer Nick would be the captain, and I could resume my place as first mate. Helen's voice interrupted my thoughts. "Let's go. The captain is ready."

I walked down the dock to the boat, and smiling at Reggie, I asked, "Captain, permission to come aboard?"

As I boarded, Reggie gave me a hug and a kiss and said, "You are always welcome aboard this vessel."

Because of the time of day, I knew that the lighthouse wouldn't be visible. But to my surprise there it was. Most of the overgrowth was gone. It was standing there in its entire splendor, reaching to the sky as if to catch a cloud. I could see that construction had been started on a new dock. Scaffolds were raised against the grand old structure, and renovation was in progress.

In amazement, I asked Helen what was going on. She had heard that someone was living there and restoring the cottage and the old lighthouse. She wasn't sure if it was to be used as a home or a museum. Whoever bought it had been working on it since early March and seemed to be doing everything alone. No one else had been seen on the island. That didn't surprise me. He didn't like strangers around. Part of me wanted to see him, but I couldn't. Was I afraid of what emotions would begin to surface again? I wasn't sure. All I knew was that I didn't want to be put to the test. *Doesn't she remember how I had tried to convince them it existed? She must remember the day we went looking for it. Apparently not. Good. I don't have to talk about it.*

Helen's voice brought me back to reality. "So I guess he really wants to be alone and maybe surprise all of us when he is done with whatever he is doing. Or he may just want to make this his very own private place. There are 'no trespassing' signs all around the island. They say this guy is very mysterious. A few people had thought that they had seen him sitting on the beach with an easel and paints on several occasions."

Hearing that last comment, I froze. I didn't hear a word Helen said from then on. What hold did he have on me and why? My body was trembling, as I realized I had had no control over my own mind and I wanted so desperately to go to him. If my marriage was to continue, I needed to go back to New York immediately and never return to Michigan again. I had one answer! He was the artist in New York. But what or who in his life made him so unable to accept and give love?

Helen noticed my uneasiness. I wanted to tell her everything and just cry until I couldn't cry any longer. Trying so hard to hold back the tears, I informed her I wasn't feeling well and needed to return to shore. My heart breaking, I wanted to see him again. How could this be happening to me once more? My life with Nick was so perfect. I really did love him very much, but this man had a hold on me I couldn't understand.

We returned to shore, and I went directly to the boat and called Nick. I told him I was ill and wanted to return to New York on the next plane. His concern only made it worse because I knew why and was unable to tell him the truth.

Nick then asked, "Exactly how do you feel? Is it possible you could be pregnant?"

I could hear the hope in his voice. If only that was the reason. But I knew it wasn't. Sadly I said, "I don't think so, but we'll find out together when I get home." How could I lie to him? He didn't deserve this.

"Just stay there. I'll fly out tomorrow. I can cancel my appointments and take a week off. We'll see a doctor there. I don't want you traveling alone if you are ill. We don't want to take any unnecessary chances."

I agreed only because I had no choice. It was either tell him the truth or continue to hide it. I needed to be alone. Being concerned, Helen and Reggie wanted to stay with me. I told them I was fine, just a little tired.

I waited a while, left the boat, and went to the park. I sat on a bench for hours, or at least it seemed that long. Thoughts of the good times my friend and I had spent together returned and so did the tears. Finally, I got up. Feeling light headed I lost my balance. Someone caught me. It was him. He held me so tightly I couldn't resist. I didn't want to. We melted into each other's arms. He wiped away my tears with his kisses. We didn't speak. Words weren't needed. Why hadn't he done this before? Had he changed his mind now that it was too late?

"I'm so sorry I didn't stop you after I got your letter. I couldn't deal with knowing you loved me. I thought being away from you would make me forget, but it didn't. I still don't know what I am feeling. I can't get close to anyone. When they get close to me, I leave. That's why I let you go."

I could see the tears in his eyes. Tears he tried to stop and hide.

"So what are you saying? You want me in your life, but you don't know why or what I mean to you?"

"Yes. I am happy when we are together, but I don't want to depend on anyone to be by my side. I have always been a loner. I can't ask anyone to share my lifestyle. I know that you make me think about my future or even if I have one. I have never done that before. I'm not ready to change. I don't know what is ahead for me."

How could I find the words I now had to say? "I need to tell you that I can't see you anymore. I still love you and always will, but you can't return that love. I married Nick this past June. I love him very much, and I can't do this to him. I have never told him about you. I tried so many times, but didn't know what to say because I never felt there was an 'us'. I needed to hear you say that you loved me, but you couldn't and I knew that. I wanted to tell you how much I loved you but couldn't risk the rejection. But then I told you all that in my letter. Please walk out of my life, and let me go."

Now was the time to ask the questions I needed answers to, and I really thought I could get the truth now. The time was right.

"Can you say you can never loved me? Who was that woman I saw you with and why did you lie to me about going out of town? Why didn't you tell me about the paintings and that you were an artist?"

"I can't answer your first question, because I don't know. How did you know I was an artist? I never told you."

"My husband, Nick, thought you were an old college friend of his named 'Bryant'. He wanted to surprise you, and we had tickets for the opening night at the gallery in New York. You, of course, weren't there. Someone had told him about your exhibit, and the only thing he knew was that the artist signed one painting with the name, 'Bryant'. All of the others just had the letter 'B'. When I saw 'Broken Promise,' I thought it was Brian and me and the promise he had made to me. Was it?"

61

"Oh, I'm really sorry you thought that. It wasn't you. I didn't mean to mislead you, but I never told you I was an artist and never expected you to see it. I decided that I didn't want to share my life story in pictures with anyone and pulled the show."

"Who are the people in the picture?"

"I can't tell you that. I am not ready to share that with anyone. Please don't ask. As for the girl you saw on the island, I'll tell you about her. I had to tell you I was going away because I needed to take care of personal affairs with her. We knew each other in college. Like you, I had a very nice relationship with her until it came time to make a commitment. I left school and disappeared from her life and life itself. No one knew where I had gone. I left and burned all bridges behind me. I made sure no one would be able to find me. And it worked until just before you saw us. She never accepted my leaving without a word. It took her a long time and many dead ends before she finally found me. She never gave up because she never stopped loving me. It is really hard for me to say those words even now. I don't know why I am so incapable of loving, but the feeling is just not there. I guess I don't know the meaning of true love. She had to hear me say the words and know that there could never be anything between us before she could go on with her life. I never knew she felt that strongly. I didn't understand. You made me understand how much I have hurt her and you. I have done a lot of thinking and soul searching lately. Now it is too late and I guess it's better this way. I don't know the answer. You say you love both your husband and me. I'm not sure that's possible."

"You won't believe this, but yes, it is possible. All I know is that when I am in your arms and you touch me, I am completely happy. I told you I loved you from the beginning and didn't understand why. It is you, the person you are when we are together. Your smile, your voice, your touch, — they're all like magic to me. I know that when I am with you, I want time to stand still and never end. That will never stop. As for Nick, he gives me all the love you can't. Our life together is wonderful. He makes me happy in a different way. I want children before it is too late. I want someone to be there for me. You can't or won't do that. Had you come to me and stopped me when I left last fall, I would have never left you and would have devoted my life to making you happy and to understand what true love was. Does it bother you that two women have loved you so?"

"I never asked either of you for that love. I told both of you that there were to be no commitments or love. Our friendship was just that — friendship with no love or strings."

"But why did you let us love you so?"

"I didn't let you. You did. For that I am really sorry. I tried to stop seeing you, but you were fun to be with. You truly made me happy, and we had fun together. I guess I realized that you wanted more than just friendship. I didn't. Or at least that's what I thought. I needed space and time away from you. I thought when you returned this summer, we could still have our time together and have fun being friends again."

"So, your way of dealing with it was to have friendship to come to a standstill instead of going forward?"

"Maybe that wasn't the right thing to say. I enjoyed being with you and talking to you. You listened to me and tried to help me, but I didn't want your help because I didn't think I needed it. I really am satisfied with my life. I thought that when you returned this summer, I would try to be a little more like you wanted me to be, and now it's too late."

"What will you do now? Run away again?"

"No, I have my island. I'm renovating the cottage and the lighthouse. It will be my home now. I'm starting to make friends on the mainland. I have my painting. Can we still be friends?"

"How can you ask me, knowing it could destroy my marriage?"

"You're right. But remember one thing. I will always be here if you need me. I can never forget you and you're a very important part of my life too."

I could see that he was sincere.

"If you do decide that you really can and do love me, please don't tell me. It is very difficult for me to walk away from you again."

I turned and walked back to the boat, leaving him standing there.

I heard him softly say, "Goodbye."

His voice had always been like velvet to me. Would I always hear it in the back of my mind? Now we must sell the boat and leave forever if I was to be free and completely faithful to Nick. If I ever told Nick the truth, I would have to tell him part of me would always love Bryant. That would surely end my marriage.

When Nick arrived the next day, I tried to convince him that I was fine and he needn't have rushed here. But he wouldn't have it any other way. He also insisted that we make an appointment with a local doctor and have a pregnancy test. As much as we wanted this, it was not the right time. I was very upset, and that would not be good for a baby.

I tried to persuade Nick to wait until we got back to New York, but he wouldn't hear of it. Maybe he was right. I really felt worse when I got up the next morning. Breakfast wasn't an option. Even the coffee made me sick. I tried to tell myself it was because of my final meeting with Bryant and the emotional goodbye. When I walked away that night, there was an emptiness that could never be filled. I also remembered that I had had several glasses of wine to relax. That wasn't good if I was pregnant.

Things didn't go well at the doctor's. My blood pressure was high and the doctor noticed my anxiety. I told him that I had never had that problem before.

After the examination, the doctor left the room. When he returned, Nick was with him. He said, "I'm sure this won't be a surprise to you. You're pregnant. That's probably the reason for the rise in your blood pressure. You need to rest and bring it down."

Nick and I looked at each other and he put his arm around me and whispered in my ear, "I knew it, and I'll bet I can tell you the exact night. Do you remember?"

"You bet I do."

The doctor cleared his throat, reminding us he was still present and suggested I stay in town for a few weeks. He said that flying back to New York was not a good idea. Just what I didn't need to hear. I couldn't tell him that returning to New York was exactly what

I needed.

I told the doctor, "I think I should return to New York with my husband. He'll worry about me here. He needs to return to work."

Nick didn't agree. "Don't worry about that, I'll have my office send all my accounts here and stay until the doctor thinks you should fly."

Listening to our discussion, the doctor decided that Nick had everything under control and that he was in complete agreement with Nick. He said, "Okay, I want to see you back in one week. We'll keep an eye on that pressure, and if it comes down, I'll let you return home."

I wasn't prepared for Nick's next suggestion. "Maybe we should consider staying here for the summer. You know how peaceful and quiet it is here, not like the noise and sounds of the big city. When I do have to go back for a day or so, you'll have Helen and Reggie right next to you, and I won't worry. Ann and Stan live across town, and it would be hard for them to keep an eye on you. I really would feel much better if you stayed here."

I wanted to insist that we return to New York as soon as possible. But what excuse could I use? All his reasons for staying here were for my best interest. I would have no choice but to tell Nick why I needed to leave; either that or I could stay and make the best of it. I had decided to stay until I felt better, and then convince Nick we had to go home.

Now that the lighthouse was visible all the time, I found it impossible to take the boat out to the bay. I used the excuse of being afraid of having motion sickness. Everyone laughed and said they didn't think so, but if that was what I thought, it was fine with them.

It was time for me to see the doctor again. Nick was waiting for an important conference call. I told him that he didn't need to go with me.

The news wasn't good. In spite of following the doctor's orders, my blood pressure was still high. He prescribed complete bed rest. He had the nurse make an appointment for the following week. I went right home and told Nick what had happened. We were both very worried.

Two days later, I was rushed to the hospital. I lost the baby. As Nick held me in his arms and comforted me he assured me that we would try again. Now there was no reason to stay. We could go back to New York. The doctor insisted I spend at least one day in the hospital. Nick went back to the boat and made arrangements for us to leave as soon as possible.

I was so tired, and that emptiness came over me again. The nurse gave me something to relax and help me sleep. I dozed off very quickly. All at once, I had that same feeling I had had in the cottage that first night. I opened my eyes, and there he was, standing by my bed, holding my hand. Was I dreaming? I couldn't keep my eyes open. I tried very hard to wake up but couldn't. I felt that touch. *Please let this be a dream and let me wake up to see Nick standing there holding my hand.* But I knew the touch was his. I always felt his touch like no other. Still fighting to wake up, I couldn't. Then I heard that velvet voice saying, "I am so sorry this has happened to you. I always wanted you to be happy and to live the life you deserve. I know how much this baby meant to you."

I finally opened my eyes, and he was gone. Or had he really been there?

I called Nick and told him to put the boat up for sale. I wanted to go home immediately. I had lost Brian and now my baby. The boat no longer held happy memories for me, only heartache. Nick understood. He was devastated losing our baby and concerned about my physical and mental state. "I'll do anything you want. I can't bear to see you so unhappy."

He was doing this for me. I knew he really wanted to stay here with the quietness of the small town and the tranquility of being on the open waters. He also had suffered a great loss. I was being selfish thinking only of myself. Unable to tell him why, I knew that selling the boat was the only way our marriage could survive.

As I lay there thinking about whether Bryant had really been here, or not. I reached for the phone. I promised myself I would never contact him again, but I had to know the truth. The phone rang several times before the answering machine came on. I couldn't leave a message. This was too important to me. I waited and called an hour later. This time I heard his haunting voice. "Hello."

"I promised myself that I would never see or talk to you again, but I need to know if you were you standing by my bedside in the hospital holding my hand."

"No, but I wish I could have been. I wanted to be there."

"How did you know I was there? Who told you?"

"I was in the grocery store, and I heard your husband telling Mae, the clerk, what had happened. I wanted to be by your side and comfort you as you, without knowing, had done for me so many times in the past. I realized how much you really do mean to me. Forget what we had. Go home with Nick, and have a good life. This sad day will pass. You'll be a mother someday."

There were a few moments of silence and I finally asked, "Will I ever see you again?"

"Only if you need to. I don't think you will. This loss will bring you and Nick closer together. You won't need me. I won't say goodbye because we will never be completely apart."

I was confused as to what he meant by that remark, but before I could ask, he hung up.

Once again, he had been my teacher. He was my friend, but not my lover. He was telling me that he loved me as much as he was capable of loving. That was all I needed to hear.

CHAPTER 10

With Nick by my side, I sat impatiently waiting for the roar of the engines of the plane. That sound would be the beginning of a new life. I let Nick know that selling the boat hurt me as deeply as it did him. The plane took off. I held Nick's hand knowing that this wasn't what Nick really wanted.

"We'll take our children to Disney World, visit the national parks, and take them to all the other places parents take their children."

He gave me a smile and nodded in agreement. How did I ever doubt my love for him? He was giving up a life I had taught him to love, no questions asked. His next remark broke my heart.

"I understand what you are feeling. Losing Brian and now the baby, there are too many bad memories here. You're right. We need a happier beginning for us and our future family."

We had a lot of plans to make when we got home. First of all, we were going to move out of the city into the suburbs. The weeks went by quickly as we put the apartment up for sale and started looking for a house. I found the perfect one — an old Victorian. It needed a little work, but on the whole was well maintained. I hired a professional to help renovate and decorate it. I focused on my marriage, new home, and our desire to start a family.

My doctor in New York assured me that the probability of miscarrying again was not likely. My health was fine, and I was in very good physical condition. I exercised daily, ate properly and generally took very good care of myself.

Three months later, we moved into our home. Nick and I were both very excited. We even had the nursery decorated in hopes of using it soon. We also had new neighbors to meet. The day we moved in, a welcoming committee arrived with gifts welcoming us into the neighborhood. Our new life was really beginning. Now all we needed was a baby.

We celebrated Thanksgiving at Ann and Stan's, as was the custom. The four of us decided to take a cruise after the Christmas season because we enjoyed the Christmas holidays and all the festivities. New Year's Eve in Hawaii sounded ideal. I started to make arrangements for our vacation, and with so many things going, I didn't have time to think about the past, only the future.

Our cruise would take us to four islands in Hawaii. Nick and I had enjoyed Hawaii so much on our honeymoon, and we wanted to go back. Ann and Stan had never been there and were eager to go. We all had a wonderful time. Memories of our honeymoon made our love stronger than ever. Especially the romantic evening walks on the beach.

A few weeks after we returned from our trip, I started to feel ill in the mornings and afternoons again. I made a doctor's appointment without telling Nick. I didn't want to disappoint him again. If I was pregnant, I wanted to make sure everything would be all right this time.

I was right. I was pregnant again, and this time everything appeared to be fine except for the morning sickness. My blood pressure was normal. On my way home, I visualized the perfect time and atmosphere to tell Nick.

When Nick came home from work, he noticed that the dinner table wasn't set. He asked if I was planning on going out for dinner.

"No. We're staying home. But tonight we're having dinner in a different room."

He had a puzzled look on his face and asked, "What are you up to?"

"Close your eyes, and don't open them until I tell you."

I took his hand and led him to the nursery. There I had set up a small table with candles, and dinner was ready.

"Open your eyes."

He looked around and picked me up. "Does this mean what I think it does?"

"Yes. The doctor said that there's nothing to worry about. I'm in excellent physical condition."

I've never seen anyone as happy as he was at that moment.

We sat for hours in the nursery making plans for the baby's future. Nick had even picked out the college. We needed to pick out names but couldn't agree on a boy's name. I thought it would be Nick, Jr., of course. A girl would be Victoria. With a little persuasion, he agreed.

I called our friends in Michigan to tell them the good news. Though still saddened by our decision to sell the boat, they continued to keep in touch. The baby was due in September, so the girls planned a baby shower. I was reluctant to go back but couldn't tell them why. I didn't want to disappoint them, so I agreed. July would be a good time. The weather would be nice, and I would stay with Helen and Reggie. Nick couldn't make the trip with me. I didn't want to go alone. But I couldn't tell him why.

The new house and getting ready for our baby made the next few months fly by. Once again the summer months were upon us, and it promised to be a very hot one. I began looking forward to the visit to Michigan where I could spend the cool nights sitting on the docks or taking an evening boat ride.

CHAPTER 11

Helen and Reggie were at the airport to pick me up. Helen and I were like two schoolgirls after summer break with so much news to catch up on. My friends were at the marina when we arrived. I had to admit that I did miss that life and the friends I had made over the years. I knew I would have to stay at the marina and away from town as much as possible. I didn't want to run into Bryant. The past was buried and had to stay there.

That night while we were visiting on the docks, the subject of the lighthouse came up. Helen gave me a curious look and asked me, "Remember when you tried to tell us about the lighthouse, that we were convinced was in your imagination?"

I hesitated as if to make it seem that I hadn't remembered, then asked, "What about it?"

"Well, you were right. Everyone can see it now. It is a showplace, but the strange thing is that no one is allowed on the island. It is strictly private property with signs all around it. The man that lives there comes to town quite often now, but he is very mysterious and doesn't like people asking about the island or lighthouse. We jokingly say we wonder what or whom he is hiding there."

She told me all this last year. Why is she telling me again? She still hasn't mentioned that day we went looking for it. Maybe she really doesn't remember. After all, it had no meaning to her.

I wanted to tell them how wrong they were about him, and that he was really a very sensitive and caring person. Finally, trying to sound unconcerned, I said, "Not spending our summers here now, I don't have an opinion. Just let him live his life as he sees fit. We all deserve that."

They agreed but still were very curious. Reggie noticed an odd look on Helen's face and glanced at me and said, "That's a rather deep comment for not having an opinion."

There was no way I could let them know what a wonderful artist he was, and that all he wanted was his privacy. I couldn't reveal that I knew him. I had to keep silent. I turned away and quickly changed the subject to my delight at being with my friends again.

The next day Helen and I went to town to pick up a few things she still needed for the shower. Of course, there was no hiding the fact that I was very pregnant. I prayed not to see him, and I didn't. I hurried Helen along using the excuse of being uncomfortable with the heat. She promised only one more stop, the grocery store.

While we were at the grocery store, I overheard Mae, the checkout girl, talking to a very pleasant middle aged woman. The woman and her daughter owned an interior decorating shop. She was telling Mae that her daughter was doing some decorating for the newly renovated cottage on the island. Mae, like everyone in the town, was curious about the mysterious man at the lighthouse. The woman remarked that he was extremely shy and polite but seemed troubled most of the time. She was telling Mae how her daughter had described the main room. It was as I had remembered, except everything there had a different meaning for me. I saw the faded furniture as old but full of character, and the room came alive whenever he smiled.

The woman also mentioned a door that was always locked. Her daughter tried to discuss the room and offered to decorate it too but was sharply told to forget it. I wanted to join the conversation but decided it was not a good idea.

Mae looked over and saw me interestingly listening to their conversation. She called me over and told me how happy she was to see that this time my pregnancy was progressing with no complications. She introduced me to the woman, Elaine, so I casually joined in. I asked her if she had helped with any of the work. She said he was very specific that no one but her daughter, Lynne, was to ever come to the island. He didn't allow her to take the usual pictures of the room to help with ideas.

Elaine said that the upstairs rooms were painted but left empty, and the only room furnished was his bedroom. The room she described seemed to fit him perfectly. There was a queen size bed with a very simple oak frame with swirled carvings resembling waves on the water. The chair and dresser matched. One wall was painted with an incredible sunrise and the opposite wall with a sunset. The sunrise was a brilliant blue sky streaked with pinks and reds. The sunset was the colors of autumn with a bright orange moon setting in a multi colored orange and blue sky. The room seemed to sum up his life. I casually inquired whom her daughter had found to paint the murals.

Elaine said, "That's the strange thing, she doesn't know. He refused to let her decorate the room until it had been painted. Since she had never seen any paint or brushes, she assumed that he had someone come in before he had hired her."

"Maybe he painted it himself," I remarked.

"She really doesn't think so. He doesn't look like an artist or someone with that much sensitivity."

I knew that he was capable of such paintings. I also knew how sensitive and creative he was. The locked room could be his studio, and all the paintings from the New York gallery might be stored there. His paintings showed so much love for the life he had chosen. The picture that I had thought was of my late husband and me, showed a love in the man's eyes like none I had ever seen. Surely that man loved that woman very deeply and if it was he, what had gone so wrong in that love? If she had died, surely he would have told me because we shared so many personal things about ourselves with each other.

The more I remembered him, the more I thought about all the things we had shared. I started remembering him with tenderness. My mind was not with the ladies and what they were saying until I heard Mae say, "Change the subject ladies. Here he comes."

My heart started to race, and I felt very weak. I had to control my emotions. He walked over to us and said hello to Elaine. She began to introduce me and as he extended his hand to shake mine, I hesitated. Slowly I extended my hand. As our hands touched, I remembered the first time I had felt that touch.

He looked at me with that smile I had loved so, and with that velvet voice said, "I'm glad to meet you. I see you're about to become a mother. Congratulations."

My hand was trembling as he spoke. I thanked him and gently pulled my hand from his. I didn't want to let go, but I had to. Coming here for the shower was a mistake, but is that why I agreed to come back? Was I hoping to see him again, just one more time? There was always that one more time. Why did I keep testing my love for him and whatever emotions he may have for me? This time it wasn't that hopeless, empty feeling. Could I finally accept this as a friendship that would always be there for me? For some reason I knew he would always be part of my life. His voice brought me back to reality.

He smiled and said, "Glad to have met you. Take care of yourself."

As he turned to leave, I said, "I've been told about your lighthouse. I have always liked lighthouses. I wonder if I could visit yours sometime?"

Why did I say that? Did it just slip out because I didn't want that to be our last meeting? Of course, he would refuse, because as Elaine had told us, he wouldn't let anyone come to the island with Lynne. He certainly couldn't agree to this in front of everyone.

Helen overheard me as she walked up. She gently pulled me aside and said, "Buying a lighthouse was your dream with Brian. Do you think you should go there? You're happy now. Don't bring back old memories. I don't think that would be in your best interest at this time, especially in your condition."

She was right. Only I knew it was not for the reasons she voiced.

I walked back to him and said, "I don't know why I made such a request. I'm sorry for being so forward."

He said, "It's okay. Lynne is coming tomorrow. Why don't you come with her if you are really interested? Give Lynne a call. Elaine can give you the phone number."

"I will be busy tomorrow. The girls are having a baby shower for me. But thank you anyway."

As he picked up his order and walked out, everyone was looking at him with astonishment. He had actually invited someone to the island.

I said, "You know how everyone treats pregnant women with kid gloves. He was afraid if he refused I would cry because I didn't get my way."

Mae looked at me and very sincerely said, "Really? Pregnant women aren't that sensitive, are they?"

"I'm joking, Mae."

With that we all laughed and Helen and I left. I was amazed. I was in total control and smiled, knowing he had actually invited me to the island. Seeing him had a peaceful affect on me.

On the way home Helen looked at me and asked what I was thinking because I was smiling. I told her I was just counting my blessings. Actually I was thinking that I was ready to fulfill my dream of being a mother. I was very much in love with my husband, and I loved my best friend. He was happy with his life, I was still a part of it, and I was content with that. I have everything I had ever wanted.

The next day, Helen had everything under control for the shower. I wanted to go with Lynne to the lighthouse. I couldn't understand why Helen was so upset about my going. She even seemed a little angry with me. Helen suggested that first I call Lynne and tell her what had happened at the store, and ask her if I could tag along. I called and found out that her mother had mentioned the incident to her. Because she knew that I had been invited, she must have felt compelled to agree.

She picked me up and introduced herself. She had an inquisitive look on her face and I knew what she was thinking. I supplied the answers before she asked. I told her about Brian and explained that we had planned on trying to buy a lighthouse when we retired, and about his sudden death. This one interested me because I couldn't find any information about it. I told her all about Nick. We talked like two old friends.

The subject came around to Bryant. Since she had taken on the job, she found herself wanting to return to the island to see him more often than he wanted her to. She started to make mistakes so she could return and rectify them. At first he was very patient and agreed each time she returned. Then he became annoyed, and told her if she was having such difficulty with the job to either send her mother or he would finish the job himself. I could relate to that side of him, but not the rudeness. He was usually so pleasant and polite that that attitude surprised Lynne also. But I understood what was happening. She was beginning to be attracted to him, and he realized it. I wanted to tell her to walk away now before she fell hopelessly in love with him. But maybe she would be the one to complete his life. Nevertheless, I couldn't say anything.

When we arrived at the island, he was sitting on the dock. I saw his surprised look at seeing me. He took my hand and asked me if I wanted a tour of the island and cottage. When he told Lynne to go inside and that he would be in later, her smile quickly vanished. I knew that she wanted to be with him. So did I.

We walked around the grounds and talked like old friends as we had done so many times before. He asked, "Are you happy?"

"Yes, I am. My life will be complete when my baby is born. You know how much this will mean to me. We talked about it many times while we were together."

"I'm really glad for you. You know that I always wanted the best for you. When all your dreams were taken away, you didn't give up. Even though you thought you had."

"Yes, I did give up. You were the one that convinced me I was special and needed to get on with my life. You kept telling me I would love again. You knew all along that I was in love with you. Why didn't it work out between us?"

"I can't tell you that. I really did try, but it just wasn't meant to be. We had a lot in common, but our differences outweighed them. I told you, I am a very simple person, with simple needs. You were so energetic and full of life. You needed someone like Nick who could give you the social life you were used to."

He still didn't really understand me or didn't want to. I told him, "But I always let you know that I could be happy in your lifestyle. You were all I needed."

"Look at your life now, and tell me you still believe that."

I knew that I couldn't tell him that. He was right. I turned to him and saw his eyes glistening in the sunlight. He tried very hard to hold back the tears, but as he turned away I could see them running down his cheeks. I wanted to take him in my arms and comfort him as he had comforted me so many times in the past. I put my hand on his shoulder. His voice cracked, "I'm right, and we both know it."

My silence was his answer. Even in his pain, he couldn't reach out to me. If he could let me walk out of his life when we were so close, how could I have expected him to act differently now?

I changed the subject and started talking about what he had done with the island and how beautiful all the flowers were. He said he had cleared the land and planted them himself. The grass was like a very thick, expensive carpet. I took my shoes off so I could feel it between my toes. He bent down and picked a white wild flower and handed it to me. I was remembering the time we had walked along the beach, and he picked a little white wild flower. Then after giving it to me, he had taken me in his arms and so tenderly kissed me. I was sure that moment was on his mind also.

He took my hand and said, "If only…" and I stopped him.

"There is no 'if only'. We each had a choice to make and you chose to walk out of my life. It really was your decision. I would have stayed with you forever at that point. Now we both have to live with our decisions. I'm happy with mine, and I'm truly sorry if you made the wrong one."

He took a step towards me, and said, "I can't tell you if I was right or wrong. I only know I'm not sure why you came into my life when you did. But it was the wrong time for me. You're part of my memories and the best part of my past. If I tell you I was wrong, then you might begin to wonder if you did the right thing. I don't want you to start doubting yourself. You have all you ever wanted. Seeing you this happy, makes me love the person you are even more. I'll always cherish our friendship."

I hesitated and finally found the courage to say, "May I ask you something?"

"Certainly, what?"

"You knew how deeply I loved you, and at times I felt you were getting to the point that you wanted me as much as I wanted you. Then you withdrew from me and I had to start all over trying to get back into your life. Why? You wouldn't explain the painting to me because it was too painful. Why didn't you just let me believe it was Brian and me."

He turned his back to me, and I could hear that velvet voice quaver. "I should have let you believe what you thought about the painting because it made you happy. It would have been the easy way out for me. Please don't ask again, because I can't tell you. It happened a long time ago. The past is buried forever. Please respect my wishes. There are times when secrets must remain just that. We both know that very well. You are married to a wonderful man, and he must never know about us. Even though we have never made love, you were in love with both of us, and he might always wonder if you really think you made the right choice."

"You're right. We have too many good memories, and I don't want to spoil that. I want to remember you as the wonderful friend I once loved very much."

When he heard the word, "once" I saw his smile fade. He quickly turned and started back to the lighthouse. When he realized that he was walking much faster than I was, he turned around. He stopped and waited for me. He apologized for his rudeness. True to form the gentleman.

I saw the sincere look on his face, knowing that he was always honest with me from the very beginning. I too always wondered why he came into my life at that particular time. The bond we share would never be broken. There are times when secrets need to remain just that, and how well I knew that.

We were brought back to reality by Lynne's voice. She seemed upset. I knew it was because she was there to see him rather than work. I was taking up her time with him. I understood her feelings.

We followed her back into the cottage, and much to my surprise the room was exactly as I had remembered it. There was the same couch, dark green with an occasional white stripe, but this one was not faded or musty. It was new. I was taken back in time, the time when that room and the furniture were part of someone's life. But whose? He explained that he wanted this room to remain exactly as it was when he first moved into the cottage.

He never took his eyes off me and watched for each reaction as he spoke. I glanced at Lynne. She appeared very uneasy. She quickly turned to us and announced she had another appointment and was running late. We didn't realize that we had spent almost two hours talking and reminiscing. We did have a lot of nice times together, for that I was grateful. I hoped that our time together today would help him move on with his life.

Lynne insisted we leave immediately. At least we didn't have time to think about our good-byes. On our walk, we had said it all. He didn't accompany us to the boat, instead he stood in the doorway and watched us depart. I knew why he stayed behind. We both did.

On the way back to the mainland, I had wished I could have told Lynne that her heart would be broken. If only I could have let her know that he was a man that you didn't merely love, but loved completely and hopelessly. She had seen in him all the things that I had, and I understood completely why she had fallen in love with him. I couldn't tell her why he couldn't return her love, because he still refused to talk about it. Not even with me, as much as he cared for me.

I got around to discussing the door that was always locked. Lynne said, "I asked for the key to the locked door, and he said that that door was never to be unlocked. That was not part of my decorating job, and he would take care of that room himself."

Of course, I had already figured out that it was his studio. I would have liked to see the paintings again, and I wondered if he was still painting. His life was in those paintings and someday they might be on exhibit again.

Back on the mainland, the ride back to the marina was uncomfortable for both of us. We had very little to say to each other. As I said goodbye to Lynne, I got the impression that she wanted it to be a permanent 'goodbye'. Trying to put her at ease, I said, "Thank you for taking me along today. I'm very glad to have met you. I don't think we will meet again because I am going home in a couple of days."

"Where is home?"

"New York."

Her face lit up with relief. I knew how much she had wanted to spend the day with him and resented me for being there. She knew that wouldn't happen again.

Maybe loving him and being near him was all she needed and couldn't bear not having him in her life. That wasn't enough for me. I could only wish her good luck knowing what was ahead for her. I wanted him to be happy or at least content. Whatever happened in his past, I hoped his relationship with me, and the decisions we both had to make wouldn't take him further into himself. I tried so hard to bring him to this point, and now I am turning away from him, knowing he would never turn away from me. I couldn't stay in his life and continue to help him. It would destroy my life.

When we reached the marina, I opened the car door and said, "Goodbye and thank you for taking me along today."

She nodded, but didn't look at me. I closed the door and she left without saying a word.

Helen came to my rescue. It was time for the baby shower when I returned. Everything was ready and the guests were all there. The theme of the shower and the nursery was bears. Bears on boats, bikes, skateboards, skis, and in every imaginable aspect.

As I looked at the tiny clothes, the little baby growing in me became more real than ever. Nick and I would try so hard to protect him or her from ever being unhappy. This baby would grow up with two loving parents. Hopefully there would be sisters and brothers.

I put my hand in the pocket of my dress, and I felt something. I took it out and found a small painting, the size of a greeting card. It was a lighthouse with a small child playing in the sand. By the lighthouse, a lady was picking wild white flowers. *When did he put it there? Why did he paint it? Was this his way of telling me how he pictured my child and me?* Once again I was filled with questions.

My mind was no longer on all the beautiful gifts my baby was receiving from all these wonderful people. I quickly put it back into my pocket. Why did he want to hold on to me? I didn't want answers anymore. I wanted to close that door forever.

When everyone had gone, I carefully took the picture out of my pocket to take a better look at it. In the left hand bottom corner was the letter "B" It was very obvious that it was not a print, but an oil painting. Would Nick study it as closely as I had and see the letter? I think he would realize whose work it was. He had been so interested in the paintings in New York. I could simply throw it away, and that would solve all my problems. No, I couldn't destroy such a beautiful work of art. It wasn't mine to destroy. It was a gift to my unborn child.

I called Nick that night and described each little article the baby had received, all except the picture. I had to figure out how to explain it and where it came from. Finding it in a little gift shop was logical. Would the secrets ever end? This time it would not be a secret. It would be the first lie.

Helen and I carefully packed all the gifts, except the picture, which I had not shown to her, took them to town and mailed them home to New York. Walking out of the post office I saw Bryant was about to enter the coffee shop. He now had a name. I hoped he wouldn't notice us, but he did.

He quickly came over to us as we got into the car. With a big smile and sincere interest, he inquired, "How did your baby shower go yesterday?"

Helen answered before I could, and he looked at me as if to say, "I'm waiting for your answer." She continued to tell him all the details, but I could see he wasn't hearing a word she was saying. Finally he said he was glad everything went so well, and that he had to go. How could I thank him for the painting without letting Helen know?

We were leaving for the airport as soon as we had dropped the package off, and there was no way I could talk to him privately. I slowly opened my purse and reached for the envelope I had put the painting in and smiled. He knew what I was trying to say and nodded and smiled. I moved my lips with a silent, "Thank you."

CHAPTER 12

Nick met me at the airport with loads of questions about our friends and the shower. I tried to answer him, but he was talking too fast and asking too many questions.

I laughingly said, "Slow down, you'll see all the gifts when they arrive in a couple of days. Stop at the camera shop and drop off the film. We can pick it up in an hour. The guys weren't at the shower, but I did manage to get a few pictures of them for you while I was there."

"You always have a plan don't you? While we're waiting for the pictures, I'll take my two girls to lunch."

"Two girls, who are we picking up?"

"We have her here with us."

"I'm not usually this slow in getting the message. You're sure 'she' and not 'he' is here?"

"Of course. No doubt in my mind."

Moments after we sat down for lunch, I amazed myself by opening my purse, and taking out the envelope. I opened it and gave the painting to Nick. He looked at it and asked where I had gotten it. I started to tell him all about Lynne, the lighthouse renovation, meeting the owner of the lighthouse at the store the day before, inviting myself to the island, visiting the lighthouse the next day, and finally finding the painting in my pocket at the shower. I couldn't believe I was really telling him the truth. It all seemed so right. No lies. The parts I chose to leave out, were still secrets and not lies.

By the time I finished my story and lunch, it was time to pick up the pictures. I could see Nick wanted to ask questions. I reminded him that the pictures would be ready and how anxious he had been to see them. Changing the subject quickly took his mind off the painting and back to the shower and our friends.

83

When we reached the house, Nick asked to see the painting again. He looked at it very closely and saw the initial in the corner. As he studied it, he began to realize who the artist was.

"Didn't you recognize this work?"

"It looks like it might be the same person, your college friend, that had the exhibit in New York. Do you really think it might be him?"

"Yes, look at the 'B' in the corner. So that is where he retreated to and if he becomes famous someday, just think what this painting will mean to the baby and us. Now that I know where he is, I'll have to get in touch with him and thank him. Maybe he'll fill me in on what he has been doing and why he left school so abruptly."

This was not what I had expected, but I never had a chance to think about the consequences. The truth just came out. "I doubt you will be able to do that because he refuses to have anyone visit the island. Lynne told me she couldn't believe he agreed when I asked to tour the island."

Nick was puzzled and asked, "Why did you ask to see the lighthouse?"

"Please don't be hurt. Remember when I told you that Brian and I wanted to buy an old abandoned lighthouse, renovate it and maybe make it our retirement home? Well, I was just curious and thought it would be nice to visit that one. I asked if I could and he said yes."

"Yes, I do remember. I know that you have a lot of nice memories of Brian, and I don't ever want you to forget them. He was part of what has made you the person you are."

He held me in his arms and we sat on the couch talking further about the painting and how we needed to have it professionally framed. I suggested we put it in the study. He said it was given to the baby, and the nursery was the room it should be in. I couldn't tell him why I didn't want to see it each time I entered the nursery. At first it upset me when I found it in my pocket, but maybe I could handle it now. Time will tell. That emotion might be replaced with the enjoyment of the beauty of the picture.

"You're right Nick, the gift was for the baby, not us."

It wasn't meant to hurt me, it wasn't given to me. It was a gift for my baby from a dear friend. He had always considered me his special friend.

July turned out to be a very hot month. The beginning of August was starting out even hotter. Ever since I had come home, Nick had been concerned about the extreme heat. I promised him I would stay in the air-conditioned house during the hot part of the days and take walks with him in the evenings when it cooled off. Nick suggested returning to Helen and Reggie's for a few weeks. He thought it might be more relaxing by the water. I declined, saying I didn't want to leave him.

"Well Catherine, you wouldn't be leaving me because I'd go with you. I need to get away for a couple of days. A week would be nice. I miss those guys. That isn't the only reason. Work has been so stressful the past few weeks, that I really need to get away, but if you don't want to go, we won't. But I would like to get away for a weekend at least."

"Nick, why don't I make reservations at a resort in the mountains for a week? That would be just as peaceful. Honey, I know you miss the gang, but I really don't want to be with a lot of people right now. I'd rather spend some time alone with you. I think that a mountain retreat would be fun."

Nick agreed that it sounded like a good plan, and was pleased that I didn't want to share him with anyone. The next day, I called our travel agent. She gave me a couple of options. That night we made our choice. Nick put his accounts in order and on hold. We left with no phones, no laptops, and no pagers. Only in case of an extreme emergency was his secretary to contact him. The resort was only a couple hours drive from our home in upstate New York.

The Victorian style hotel was nestled among hundreds of trees creating complete shade. If you wanted sun, the pool was the only place to get it. The hotel was painted a deep burgundy and trimmed in gold and orange. True Victorian colors. The suite we had reserved was beautiful. Our rooms had been done in the same colors. There were carvings of flowers and leaves on the bronze doorknobs. In the sitting room there was a writing desk with a fancy feathered pen, leather trimmed ink blotter, and a small Tiffany lamp. Ornate armoires served as closets in the bedroom. Hanging from the keyholes of the dressers, were tasseled keys. The floral mosaic pattern of the bathroom floor matched the wash bowl and pitcher on a little stand. Small corked bottles of rosewood and lavender water add the right touch.

This vacation seemed to do wonders for both of us. Nick was more relaxed. I had noticed that he had been stressed out lately and suggested he turn some of his accounts over to the others in the office. He agreed to consider it.

We woke early one morning and decided to take a walk around the grounds before breakfast. Nick said he wasn't hungry and only wanted coffee. That wasn't like him. He had always been adamant about proper nutrition. We had only walked a short way when he wanted to turn back, so we returned to the hotel. Since it was a very humid morning, I really didn't mind cutting our walk short.

We had brought a few books on parenting with us, and he wanted to relax and do a little reading. He suggested we read them together and treat ourselves to room service for lunch. When lunch arrived, he merely picked at his. I began to worry.

I knew Nick had been under a lot of pressure at work, but this was not at all like him. I suggested that he relax and take a nap. He agreed, but only if I would lie beside him even if I didn't feel like sleeping.

When he woke, he was feeling worse. He wasn't merely tired, something was obviously wrong. I called the front desk and requested the phone number of the local doctor. The only doctor was at least twenty minutes away, if he was even available. I decided not to wait. I explained the situation to the desk clerk. He suggested that we go directly to the hospital, immediately. The hotel limo and driver were available. The driver came to the room with a wheelchair.

Seeing that I was very pregnant, the driver thought I was about to deliver. I informed him that it wasn't me, so he could relax. I had no intentions of delivering my baby in the back of the limo. That relieved his anxiety a little until he glanced over at Nick. He realized he was having difficulty breathing and was in discomfort. He got on the phone. He alerted the hospital of the problem and that we were on our way.

The cardiac team was waiting for us as we drove up to the emergency entrance. Suddenly, it all came back, the nightmare of that morning with Brian on the boat. I knew for the sake of my unborn child and my husband that I had to keep as calm as possible.

They wheeled Nick into a room, and a doctor approached me. Thinking he was there to ask questions about Nick, I began telling him what had happened earlier that day. He assured me, "The team is taking care of your husband. I'm here to check on you. Are you feeling any discomfort or pain?"

"I think I'm all right. I want to be with my husband. I promise that if I do feel that there may be a problem, I'll let you know immediately. I don't want anything to happen to our baby."

The nurse in admitting asked if there was anyone I needed to get in touch with. I was very thankful for her concern and gave her Ann's phone number. Ann and Stan would want to know and be here. I needed them by my side.

I had to do all I could to control my anxiety. I felt as if my world was once again crashing in around me. I had to get hold of myself and pray. I had never felt so alone in my life as I did at that moment. Just when I thought I no longer could keep holding on, the nurse came in to tell me Ann and Stan were on their way and would be here within the hour.

The doctor kept me informed as to Nick's progress. They had him stabilized, and were monitoring his heart. He would let me know the results of the EKG as soon as the team had finished. He seemed to be resting a little more comfortably. The doctor said that they had him on oxygen to help with his breathing. That was standard procedure, so I shouldn't be alarmed. I had no idea how long it had been since we had arrived at the hospital. The doctor that had been concerned with my condition suggested that I see Nick for a few minutes and then try to get some rest.

I was totally exhausted at that point. Too many memories were coming back that I had tried so desperately to forget. I slowly walked into the room, and as I looked at Nick, my only thought was of him. The doctor assured me Nick was out of danger and would be fine. He hadn't suffered a heart attack, but had a very strong warning. He would know more in the morning. Ann and Stan arrived as I was on my way to the room that had been prepared for Nick and me. I fell into their arms sobbing uncontrollably.

"Ann, it was awful, I couldn't get the memory of that day on the boat out of my mind. I was so afraid I would lose Nick too."

"Honey, everything will be fine. We spoke to the doctor before we came to you, and he assured us that Nick would be okay. Now you need to get into that bed and think only of that baby."

Without resistance, I gave her the key to our room at the hotel. They could spend the night there and bring me the things I would need the next morning. I wouldn't leave that hospital until Nick was released.

When the doctor had finished all the necessary tests, Nick was taken his room. I sat by his bed holding his hand. I couldn't sleep. Nick was very tired but kept trying to talk. I persuaded him to get some sleep and that I'd be there and we'd talk later. I finally fell asleep in the chair. I don't know how long I'd been sleeping. The nurse came in and gently woke me. "He is doing fine. You need to get into that bed we brought in for you and get some real sleep. It's more comfortable than that chair."

She was right. It didn't take me long to fall asleep. I really didn't know how long I'd been sleeping. I realized someone was holding my hand. I knew that touch so well. I heard that haunting voice that never really left me, "This will pass and the three of you will start a new life soon."

How did he know? How did he get here so soon? I was afraid to open my eyes. When I did, no one was there. The touch was gone. Nick was asleep. Oh please, don't let the dreams start again. Why? Why, now?

The next morning Ann and Stan arrived bright and early. They were by my side when the doctor gave us the good news. "Your husband will be fine. This was an early signal for him to change a few things in his lifestyle. Is there something besides his work that might have contributed to this?"

"Not that I can think of. The only thing he complained about was stress at work. That's why we took this vacation."

The doctor said he would release him late that day, but wanted us to stay in town for at least another week. He suggested that we finish our vacation. That wasn't a problem. It would be good for both of us. We wanted some time to enjoy each other, joking about the fact that we wouldn't be alone much longer.

Stan and Ann left when Nick was released from the hospital, confident that Nick would be fine. We did ask them to stay for a few more days, but they declined.

I prayed each night that the dream wouldn't reoccur, but it did. The words, "I will always be there if you need me," kept coming back. I didn't need him. I had Nick and soon our baby.

When we got back home, I called Helen and Reggie and told them what had happened. They of course, wanted to know if I needed anything. I thanked them and said we were doing fine, and if they wanted to visit they were always welcome. Since the baby was due within the next month, they would wait until the baby arrived. Then Helen would come to help when I got home from the hospital.

I tried not to ask this question, but I had to. "What's new around there? Any news about the mystery man on the island? How's the renovation on the lighthouse coming?"

Helen sounded reluctant to answer but finally did. She really didn't know much about it, except that it seemed he had been gone for the last month. Nothing more had been done around the place. Lynne was upset because he left without a word, and there was more work that needed to be done. Stunned, I kept saying "Okay" as if I was listening to her. But I wasn't listening to a word she was saying. I finally managed, using the excuse that Nick was calling me, to regretfully end our conversation. I knew that I needed to talk to Bryant.

I was about to do something I hadn't done since leaving Michigan. I was going to call him. The number was burned into my memory. I dialed it, praying he wouldn't answer. If he did, I would hang up. I needed to know if he was there. But if he didn't answer, I wouldn't know where he was. He could be outside, in town or away. Then I prayed he would answer. I called every hour for the entire day. No answer. The answering machine was turned off.

The next day, I started calling again. At last, around noon, he answered. I tried to hang up, but couldn't. His voice once again was something I had to hear. He said hello several times, but I couldn't answer. If I said I had the wrong number, he would have recognized my voice.

Finally, I said, "Hello. Please don't be angry, I had to call. I need to tell you what has happened."

He interrupted and said, "Why would I be angry? I always like hearing from you. What do you need? Are you okay? Did you have the baby?"

"No, I'm due in a month. I'm fine. It's Nick. We thought he suffered a heart attack, but it was stress."

"I'm really sorry to hear that. Is he okay?"

"Yes. He needs to lessen his workload and take the stress from his life. The first night that Nick was in the hospital, a strange thing happened. I was sleeping and I could feel your hand holding mine. I could hear you talking to me. I couldn't tell if it was a dream because I was so totally exhausted. I tried to open my eyes, but couldn't. When I did you were gone. Were you there?"

"No. I wasn't there. You must have been dreaming. I told you that I would always come to you if you needed me. It was wrong for me to tell you that. That's Nick's place now. I don't know why that happened. I'll do whatever you want to help you."

"There really isn't anything you can do. I need to work through this myself. I have to get you out of my mind and life forever and I don't know how. It's my problem."

"No. It's my problem too. I can't get you out of my mind and I think about you all the time. I tried to have a relationship with Lynne, but it didn't work. I have hurt her also. I shouldn't be telling you this. I miss our talks and being with you. I miss having you tell me that everything will work out and helping me with the little things in life that never meant anything to me until you. I have no right telling you this. I can't do to Nick what…"

Then silence.

"Why did you stop? What are you trying to tell me? Please stop shutting me out. I still want to help you."

"You can't help. This is something I have to deal with on my own. I need to know that you are happy. The rest will take care of itself."

"But your way is denial. No matter what happens, I will never call you again. My relationship with you has brought me much happiness, but even more heartache. I realize that now. You wanted me when you knew it was safe. You knew that if you never told me how you really felt, I'd always wonder and you would always have that hold on me. Why, what was the point? I know you won't tell me. Well, I don't want to know anymore."

I hung up without hearing his response. Suddenly I became angry. He enjoyed having this hold on me. He was a selfish person who only wanted what pleased him. I think he enjoyed having women fall in love with him and knowing, for some reason, he was irresistible to them. Why did he have so little regard for their feelings? That was part of his secret and I no longer cared. He always made me feel that I needed him. Well, I don't.

Nick would never know what had happened. At this time in his life all he needed was a loving wife and his soon-to-be born child. As for Bryant, he would never know the joy of a loving wife or a family. I pitied him. When love turns to pity, it's over.

CHAPTER 13

September finally arrived and my due date, the thirteenth, neared. Nick was doing great. We didn't find out the sex of our baby because we both agreed that was part of the whole mystery of birth. It really didn't matter; all we wanted was a healthy baby. I was completely at peace with myself now.

I gently woke Nick with the news that it was time to go to the hospital. This time would be different; I'd be bringing our baby home. We arrived at the hospital at eight a.m. and at eleven a.m. our daughter came into the world, weighing six pounds and measuring eighteen inches long. She was perfect. She looked like a little angel. Her hair was as dark as her father's was, and her complexion was light like mine. We named her Victoria.

It all happened so quickly, that her godparents Ann and Stan didn't get there before she entered the world. As Ann held Victoria for the first time, in her eyes I could see the joy she felt for me, and then the sadness she felt not having a child of her own.

When we took Victoria home, we sent out announcements to our friends in Michigan. I didn't care if he would find out about the birth. It no longer mattered. Helen called to let us know that everyone sent his or her love and well wishes.

The congratulation cards had started to arrive. As I opened them and read each one with love, I placed them on the table in the living room so Nick could see them when he got home from work. I continued to open them, when I noticed one had no return address. Curiously I opened it right away. Inside was a portrait of woman holding a baby in her arms. I was the woman. This time, I would not show it to Nick. I tore the envelope and the painting into little pieces and threw it away.

Why did he continue to do this to me? My pity now turned to

anger. Anger at the thought that he wanted to continue hurting me. He had said he would never walk out of my life and would always be a part of it. He might think he was still a part of my life, but he was wrong. I found it hard to understand why he needed to hold on to what never was. I no longer had that need. Victoria has replaced his touch and his smile.

Nick recovered completely, and our daughter was all it took. He came home from the office every night by five-thirty. Late nights and weekends belonged to his family, not the company.

Watching him rocking Victoria and softly telling her how her life would be, I quietly looked up and thanked God for all he had given us. I sometimes felt Brian's presence telling me it was good to see me this happy again. I even felt his touch at times while I was holding Victoria. The two men I had truly loved and who loved me made me the person I really was.

Looking back on the days on the island, I realized how much a part Bryant had also played in shaping my life. In the beginning the island, lighthouse and 'Friend' didn't appear to be real. I only knew my love for him was very real. Now all of that all seemed hundreds of years ago. Time and distance had helped, but Nick and Victoria were the real reasons for my happy existence. I needed to remove all reminders, and I managed to take the painting out of the nursery without Nick noticing.

Ann and I went on a shopping trip, and Victoria was left in the loving care of Dad and Godfather, Stan. We felt that since she was only three months old, they couldn't do too much to spoil her. Moms can seem to say 'no' to little girls easier than dads can. Ann gave me a sly glance, "Give her some time and then watch out for that credit card when she asks Dad to take her shopping."

Ann and Stan wanted to be part of Victoria's first Christmas, and rightfully so. If it hadn't been for them, she wouldn't be here.

Christmas shopping this year had a whole new meaning. At first I wondered what could you buy a baby that little. But I soon I realized there was no end to my shopping. She, of course, needed everything that caught my eye screaming, "Buy me."

Nick did a little shopping on his own. He bought the biggest tree he could find, sparing no expense. Ceilings in old Victorian homes are very high, so the tree had to reach it.

Nick and I had so much fun decorating the tree that year. Everything was so different now. When the tree was almost completed, Nick took out the painting that I had carefully hidden in the closet and put it on the tree.

"Why did you put that painting on the tree?"

"It fits with all the other nautical decorations from our friends. Why did you take it down?"

"I didn't realize that you had noticed."

"Yes, I did. I didn't mention it because I felt you had your reasons."

"I do. The room is done in bears and it seemed out of place. Had there been a toy bear in the child's hand or on the beach next to the child, it would have fit into the room perfectly. If you like, you could put it in your study. I think that would be a good place for it."

"No. It's Victoria's. We'll put it away in her scrapbook. She can decide what she wants to do with it when she is old enough to decorate her own room."

"You're right. I should have mentioned that I took it down. You always have the solution."

I began to wonder how he had found it. I had hidden it very carefully, I thought. Somehow Bryant always seemed to intrude in my life. It no longer was only my life he was affecting, but my family's. Would he always find a way to be in our lives?

I soon forgot all about the incident and got caught up in the spirit of baking, sending out Christmas cards, shopping and planning the party for all our friends. We invited Helen and Reggie to our place for the holidays. They were looking forward to the New Year's Eve party, but regretted missing Victoria's first Christmas. It would be so nice seeing them again.

With everything going as perfect as possible, and nothing could spoil our ideal world. Nick had come home from work earlier than usual and announced we were meeting Ann and Stan in the city for dinner. Stan had been given four tickets to a showing of 'Winter

Beach' at the local art gallery. His next announcement left me in shock.

"It sounds as though this artist could be Bryant. Hey, wouldn't that be nice? We can personally thank him for the painting he gave Victoria."

Nick was so excited about the whole situation. How could I stop this evening? I couldn't go through that again.

"Nick, we can't get a sitter on such short notice. We'll just have to call and cancel right now so they can find someone else to go."

"I have that covered. We're are taking her with us. There's no reason she can't go out for an evening with her parents and godparents. Come on, it'll be fun. We'll take pictures of her first evening dining out, and she can meet a possible soon-to-be famous artist."

Nick's enthusiasm was overwhelming. I couldn't find a reason or argument in my defense. Using an excuse of not feeling well would only make him worry about me. That wasn't fair. Neither was the situation. Maybe I was a little too apprehensive. There might be no reason to be.

"I can see how much this means to you. You're right. It will be a nice memory to put in her scrapbook."

If he only knew that wasn't a memory I wanted, and how hard it would be for me to get through the evening. I wanted that man out of our lives. Why was I destined to always have an obstacle in the way of my happiness?

Dreading the evening, I took my time dressing. Nick jokingly reminded me to hurry up and stop acting like a schoolgirl trying to pick the right outfit for her first date.

It was Victoria's first evening out not mine. She was all ready to go. He had stopped at the children's store on his way home and had gotten her a new dress just for the occasion.

Ann and Stan had selected a Greek restaurant that had recently opened. The meal was very good. I tried to make dinnertime last as long as possible. When it was time to go, I procrastinated trying to delay the inevitable. They assured me if I liked this place so much we would return another time, but they were anxious to see the exhibit. I had to face my fears. "Respect and learn from your fears," Brian's words were going around in my head. What is there to respect and learn from this?

Ann was waving her hand in front of me, "Earth to Catherine. What planet are you on?"

"What? Oh, I'm sorry. I was thinking I should give the baby a bottle before we leave so she won't fuss at the gallery and disturb anyone."

"Catherine, what is the matter? You just gave her one before we had our dinner. Are you all right?"

"Yes. We've never kept her out this late. It will be past her bedtime when we get home and I hope it doesn't throw her off schedule."

"Honey, if she gets off schedule, I'll take care of her during the night."

"No, I'm sorry for being such a pain. I'll take care of it. Maybe we won't have to worry about it anyway."

"That's my girl. I should say girls. Let's enjoy the evening and worry about the night hours if we need to."

I will make it through this evening because of the wonderful man by my side. We drove up to the gallery and took the valet service. I would have preferred to walk— I needed the air— but we had the baby and the air was rather cold and damp.

CHAPTER 14

If Bryant were in character, he wouldn't be there. There was no letter of apology on the door. Maybe one would be inside. No such luck. Now, I had to face him. I might be able to avoid him. That could have been a possibility, but not likely to happen. There seemed to be quite a large crowd attending. I knew how anxious Nick had been to find out if this artist was his old college friend, and if it was, to see him after all those years.

We wandered around for about a half an hour. The paintings were exquisite. It was a completely different exhibit than the first one we had seen. All the paintings were new and depicted winter on the island with the windows of the majestic lighthouse painted with snow instead of dirt as I had first seen them.

Ann, Stan and Nick talked non-stop and studied each picture with much care. I kept silent. Ann finally leaned over and whispered to me, "Catherine. What's wrong? Are you ill? You're so distant tonight."

"No, everything is fine."

"I know there is something wrong. Is Nick okay, or is he having health problems again?"

"Oh, no. He's fine.

"You haven't been yourself lately, and I know you well enough to know there is something bothering you. Please tell me. I want to help."

"Ann, I wish I could tell you, but I can't. Please trust me. Nick and I have never been as close as we are now. The problem is personal and doesn't include my family. It is something I need to work through myself. I know I can, and maybe someday I'll find the need to tell you, but I hope that never happens."

With that Ann looked at me very puzzled and knew that she

couldn't pry any longer.

Then suddenly, there he was. A crowd had gathered around him. He was answering their questions about one of the paintings. He turned his head and saw us. He quickly stopped talking, excused himself and walked towards us. He extended his hand to Nick and said, "I think I know you, don't I?"

"Well, if you're Bryant, yes you do."

"Yes, I am, and I do remember you."

"Bryant, I would like you to meet my wife Catherine and my baby daughter Victoria. These lovely people are Ann and Stan our dear friends."

Caught up in the excitement of the evening, Nick momentarily forgot about my visit to the lighthouse and the picture Bryant slipped into my pocket during that visit. Then with a look of sudden realization, he put his hand in mine and said, "That's right, you've already met my wife when she invited herself to your island. That's my Catherine. Not a shy bone in her body. She has the ability to make perfect strangers her dear friends within minutes of meeting them. Never a dull moment with her."

"Oh, yes. I remember that day. What a small world. Imagine you being the wife of an old acquaintance. It's nice to see you again. I hope you enjoyed the tour as much as I did giving it."

Then he held out his hand. I looked into his eyes and knew I couldn't let him touch me. He reached over, took my hand and held it very gently. I knew I couldn't resist without trying to explain to the others why I refused his handshake. As he slowly released my hand, I smiled and reached for Nick's arm.

He turned to Nick and asked if he could see the baby. She was sleeping in Nick's arms, and he carefully turned her around. Bryant gently touched her cheek and said, "She is very beautiful. She looks like her mother."

With great difficulty, I managed to say, "Thank you."

He then turned to Ann and Stan and told them he was glad to have met them and hoped that they were enjoying the exhibit.

He looked at me with those deep, serious eyes, and I turned away.

I told Nick to give the baby to me so he could go off with his friend and visit. I said, "The two of you must have a lot to catch up on, and we'll be fine. We'll catch up with you later."

I walked away holding Victoria very close. My heart was beating so rapidly that I thought it would explode. I quickly gave the baby to Ann, sat on the nearest chair and said, "I must have had a little too much wine at dinner. I don't feel too good. Please excuse me for a minute."

Ann suggested we get Nick and leave, but I refused to ruin his reunion with his old friend.

"I'll sit here and the two of you take Victoria and enjoy the exhibit. I'll catch up with you shortly."

Ann was full of questions, but took Victoria and gave me a very troubled look.

It took me a while to compose myself. I tried very hard to keep my mind on my interpretations of what the artist was trying to say. I knew exactly what he meant in each one. I knew, oh too well.

I wondered why there were no paintings from the first exhibit. All of the pictures were winter scenes of the lighthouse and the beach. The one I found particularly interesting was of the snow-covered ground. A blanket with a heart in the middle of it was lying by the shore but not covered with snow. In another corner was a sand pail decorated with little white wild flowers.

I heard his voice behind me. "This one seems to have you puzzled. Let me explain it to you."

I turned quickly. "I didn't know that you and Nick were back. You startled me. Where's Nick?"

"Nick's with your friends. I offered to look for you. Do you want me to tell you what I was saying here?"

"Please try to understand that I'm not trying to be rude. I can't have you here with me. I had put you out of my heart and mind and it worked until now. You must know what affect you have always had on me."

"But the last time we met at the island, I thought you were comfortable with our friendship. When you showed me the picture as you left for the airport, you were smiling. What's different now? Tell me what you want."

"No. You tell me what you want. I thought it would be the last time I would ever have to face you and this feeling. Haven't you heard anything I've said to you? You really don't understand me, do you?"

He reached over to take my hand. I stepped away. Just then Nick and the others came up to us. Bryant and I stood there looking at each other. Nothing more could be said. Bryant glanced at me and then at the picture and said, "I was about to explain this one to your wife. The snow is my life. The heart on the blanket is the heart of a dear friend. The blanket is her love. She gave me her heart and covered my cold existence with her love. The flowers on the sand pail were the only things of beauty I had ever given her. The snow-covered windows represent my not letting anyone see into my heart. The sun shining through the dark winter sky is her love always shining on me. The broken ice on the water is my cold heart broken when I realized what she was trying to tell me. Now don't ask any questions about the person who inspired this, I won't tell you. You can see that she was a very special person to be remembered in this way."

Nick, Ann and Stan just stood there looking at the picture in awe. It was very evident this story had touched them. *Oh, Nick, what are you thinking at this moment?* If he knew the truth, his world would come crashing down. He knew how much I loved him, but would he understand or forgive me for keeping my friendship with Bryant from him? Had I told Nick in the beginning, I still would have chosen him. Would I be able to convince him of that now?

I wondered how I could have loved a man who keeps coming into my life for the soul purpose of keeping me in his life. Why? He admitted his heart had been broken, talked about the love of this woman for him, but never really professed his love for her. He appreciated all she had tried to teach him. Was he telling me how sorry he was for not being able to accept and return my love?

"Honey, are you with us or lost in that painting?"

Nick's words gave me the opportunity to let Bryant know how I felt. "No. I'm here with you and always will be."

I didn't look at Bryant because I didn't want to see what affect—if any— my answer had on him.

With that I turned to Ann, took the baby and told them we needed to go. We had kept Victoria out much too late. Nick and Bryant shook hands and agreed to meet for lunch. I said nothing, not even good-bye. Nick was so pleased at seeing his old friend, he didn't notice.

We said our good-byes to Ann and Stan, and as I got into the car to leave, I could see Bryant at the door of the gallery watching us.

On the drive home, Nick suggested that I join them whenever a luncheon date was set. I refused with the excuse that they had their memories of their college days. Since I wasn't part of that, I would sit there with nothing to say being very bored.

"You with nothing to say, Catherine? I find that hard to believe."

With a loving poke to his arm I replied, "Very funny."

CHAPTER 15

Victoria had been the perfect baby throughout the entire evening. When we got home, I got her into her pajamas, and Daddy fed her her bottle. He rocked her and sat there for a while after she had fallen asleep. He looked at her and then glanced at me. He said, "How lucky we are. I feel sorry for Bryant. He obviously had had a bad relationship with someone he loved very much."

Oh Nick, you are so wrong about him. He's incapable of loving and he only wants this person now because he doesn't need to make a commitment to her.

I didn't know how I was going to end the renewed friendship between them, but I had to and as soon as possible.

The baby didn't wake during the night, but I did. The dream came back. This time there was a faceless man and a stranger standing next to me. I asked the stranger, "Why is he faceless?"

The stranger answered, "The face is whomever you see there. If you can't see anyone, you're undecided whose face it should be."

"No. That isn't true. I know whose face is there. I can put a face there. Maybe not in my dreams but in my life I can. It's Nick's. Please let me see it."

"I can't do that. Only you are able to do that."

Once again I woke up crying, and I reached out for Nick. He wasn't there. My heart began beating rapidly. I jumped up and ran to the living room. His chair was empty. I ran through the house calling his name. He came running out of the nursery, and I ran into his arms trembling and crying uncontrollably. I tried to tell him about the dream and the fear I had had when I woke and found him gone, but I couldn't. I managed to tell him that I had had a bad dream, and that I panicked when I couldn't find him.

He looked at me and said, "I know what you were thinking, and it won't happen again. Please try to forget that day. I'm trying so hard to help you, but I don't know what to do or say. I wish I could understand why this is happening to you. Is there something you need to tell me about that day or the night before Brian died? Is there something you want to remember?"

"No, please just be by my side always. This will pass. I'm sure of it."

"I know Brian's promise still haunts you, and all I can say is I intend to see my daughter grow up and make us grandparents. Promises can unintentionally be broken. Futures can be planned."

Until tonight, I was unable to picture Bryant's face, his smile, hear his voice or feel his touch. Now it was all so clearly back. Was my guilt the reason for this? I needed to talk to someone. But who would understand? Ann seemed to be the only one I might be able to trust. I needed to do something and soon. Would Ann understand?

The next few days were more than I could bear. I tried to hide my problem from Nick, but he sensed something was very wrong. He knew that the dream was reoccurring and tried not to pressure me about it. Finally he suggested that I see someone who might possibly help me. I got very upset.

"Are you suggesting I see a psychiatrist?"

"I'm only saying that you need help with whatever is troubling you, and I can't seem to help you. I was reading about depression that some women get after childbirth. It's nothing to be ashamed of. It happens. Honey, you really need to find out what's wrong. Victoria and I need you very much. We need our happy mom back."

"Nick, you're right. Has it been that obvious? I really need to think of you and Victoria, not myself. I promise to make an appointment within the next few days. I'll call our doctor and explain the situation to him. If he feel he can't help me, I'll ask him to refer me to someone who can."

"I'll let you do this on your own until you ask for my help, and I trust you will ask if you need to."

"Nick, I'll always need you. Right now, I need you more than ever."

He took me in his arms. I began to cry. I couldn't stop the tears and I wanted to, oh how much I wanted to. I prayed, "Please make them stop." It felt as if I wanted to die. What was happening to me? I couldn't remember crying that hard when I had lost Brian. I needed to end this. I had Victoria and Nick to think about.

"It breaks my heart to see you like this. Please call the doctor today."

"I will as soon as the doctor's office opens. I have to admit I can't do this alone. I need help."

"You're not alone and never will be."

"I know, but…"

"Don't say any more. You'll accept my help when you're ready. We'll get through this together. Will you be okay if I leave for work now, or do you want me to take the day off?"

"I'll be fine. Really."

I kept my promise to Nick and called the doctor as soon as his office opened. Our doctor recommended a friend of his, Dr. Sterling. I called Dr. Sterling's office to make an appointment. Fortunately, there had been a cancellation that day, and he would be able to see me at two. On the way to his office, I began to have second thoughts. *How much am I willing to reveal?* It didn't matter, this was something I had to do.

Dr. Sterling was very nice and quickly put me at ease. I told him that I had been very depressed the past few weeks and needed to talk to someone. He understood and said a lot of new mothers go through that. "No, not this," I wanted to say.

I started from the beginning. As my story unfolded, I didn't know if I could go on, but I found it easy to tell all. At least, all I chose to tell.

He said, "What do you think your problem is?"

"Whether or not I should tell Nick about my friendship with Bryant."

"We'll decide that when we have decided if that is the real problem. Is it keeping that friendship a secret or that you still love this man? This is what we have to determine. You want the answer very much and that's a good sign. You won't try to hide from the truth."

The first meeting went very well. My next appointment was the following week, and I was looking forward to it. I was hoping it could have been the next day. I had felt a lot better when I left the office. It helped a great deal sharing that with someone after all this time and knowing that it was still a secret.

Nick came home from work and didn't ask about the first session. I knew he wanted to but was waiting for me to decide when the right time would be. After dinner he wanted to get the baby ready for bed so I could relax. He rocked her to sleep. I was grateful to him for letting me have my privacy on this matter.

I waited until we were in bed before bringing up the subject. I told him how comfortable I felt with Dr. Sterling and believed he would be able to help. I wasn't ready to tell him what we had discussed. He didn't ask. He held me very close but said nothing. I wanted him to make love to me, but hesitated. It would be unfair to him at this time.

"Nick, you will never know how much I really love you, especially now."

"Yes I do, and I have never wanted you as much as I do at this moment."

I melted into his body. It was so natural and unplanned. It just happened. The only thing on my mind was that the man I love was making love to me. I was sure the dream wouldn't be back that night.

That turned out to be the most restful night I had had in weeks. No dreams, no fears. I almost felt another session with Dr. Sterling wasn't needed. Maybe confiding in someone was all I needed. I was going to call and cancel my appointment. At breakfast Nick said, "That first session did wonders for you, and I'm sure that after a few more you will be as good as new."

"I don't think I need to go back. Everything seems to be falling into place since last night. By the way, thank you for an incredible experience."

"Thank you. But you still should see the doctor. Let him decide if you're ready to stop after one session and one night of... Are you really going to tell him about that?"

"Well, you won't be there to blush. I think he should know."

"I'd like to be there to see if you can tell him without blushing. I know you, and you'll have a hard time saying the words. Am I right?"

"No. I want him to know it was part of my therapy even though that wasn't his prescription."

Beaming, Nick kissed me goodbye and went off to work. His wife was on her way back.

I was confident that after the next session, I would tell Dr. Sterling that I didn't need to return, but it wasn't that easy. I should have cancelled like I had planned. His first words after I told him about my experience were, "Who were you making love to, Nick or Bryant?"

"Nick of course. Why do you ask?"

"Nick because he was there or because he was the substitute?"

"I resent that. How could you suggest that?"

"I'm not suggesting anything. I'm just asking."

"Well, you're wrong, I wasn't thinking of Bryant at all. In fact, I put him out of my mind until you mentioned him."

"Now how do you feel? Who are you thinking of?"

"I don't know. You have me confused. I was fine until I came here. I'm leaving. You aren't helping. You just destroyed the progress I made."

"No. I didn't destroy anything. If it was real, it is still there."

"I'm ending this session early and going home. I will call you if I think I should come back next week. Sharing my secret helped. I really think I'm going to be okay."

"Please think this over. Remember, if you need me just call, and I will leave your appointment open for next week. I would like nothing more than for you to have solved your problem."

I left the office resenting what he had asked me. I couldn't tell Nick anything about what had happened. He wouldn't ask just like before. He would wait until I was ready to talk. I didn't tell him, and he didn't ask.

CHAPTER 16

In two weeks it would be Victoria's first Christmas. I buried myself in the last preparations of the Christmas party for our friends and Nick's associates. The party was going to be a success, I would see to that. Everything was going along as scheduled and the dreams had stopped.

I cancelled my appointment, and the doctor was disappointed. He thought I hadn't made enough progress, nor had everything under control. He was wrong. Being able to tell someone about Bryant made it all real, not a dream. At times I still felt he wasn't real and I tried to tell myself he wasn't. But he was and now Dr. Sterling also knows that.

Nick was very supportive about my decision. He did say he hoped I had done the right thing and he had faith in me. That was all I needed, his support, his love and our daughter. He knew how much I loved the holidays and that would also help.

The holiday season was fast approaching. Then one evening, Nick was reading the newspaper after dinner, and he said, "Wow! I told you that people someday would see what a wonderful artist Bryant is. Here is a full-page article about him with pictures. Come here. I want you to read this."

I quickly refused saying, "I have to finish wrapping the gifts I bought today. Christmas is too close. I don't want to get behind. Put it on the table. I'll get around to it later."

Nick had gone to bed. I finished my project. I picked up the paper and without reading it threw it into the fireplace.

When I got into bed Nick was still awake. He obviously wanted to talk. He said, "I was thinking about the exhibit we saw and how glad I am that Bryant is doing so well. Didn't you wonder why he wouldn't tell us who inspired that wonderful painting of the blanket with the heart on it?"

"I really wasn't paying much attention to the story he was telling because I was concerned about getting Victoria home. I'm sure it was merely a story to make the painting more interesting and draw a bigger price. After all, it would hold everyone's interest if there was a mystery woman involved."

"Catherine, you're such a romantic. I can't believe you said that. Do you really think he was making that up? He seemed so sincere."

"Well, I really don't care one way or another. Let's get some sleep. Tomorrow is a very busy day for me."

After a few minutes of silence I was starting to drift off. Nick inquired, "By the way, did you get to read the article in the newspaper?"

"No. I forgot about it. Where did you put the paper?"

"It's on the table by the fireplace."

"Oh, no. The fire was almost out, and I wanted to keep it going for a while longer so I threw the paper on the logs. I'm sorry. Oh well, you at least got to read it, and that's all that matters."

"I'll try to pick up another paper tomorrow for you."

"Don't bother. I'm really too busy these days to read the newspaper. I haven't read it in weeks. I rely on you to tell me all the news, and you do. Now go to sleep."

Nick kissed me good night and rolled over. It only took a few minutes for both of us to fall asleep.

I was standing there holding a paintbrush in my hand. A stranger was standing next to me whispering in my ear, "You have the brush and the power to paint a face on the man standing next to you."

I raised my hand and as it reached his face, I woke to the sound of Victoria crying. Nick quickly got up and went to her room. I wanted to go right back to sleep to finish the dream. But it didn't happen. I lay there for hours wanting so desperately to finish the dream by painting Nick's face on the man next to me thus ending the dreams forever.

The next morning Nick noticed that I was totally exhausted. He asked if I had been taking on too much for the holidays. I assured him I was okay and that the festivities were what I needed. The expression on his face told me he was trying very hard to believe me.

In the past I had always had to see Bryant one last time, and that was always a mistake. Then he began to enter my life, and I had no choice. My mind began to wander. *With some luck, all the publicity he was getting might make him retreat as he did before. Maybe his old college love would turn up and he'll run away again. Nick remembered the article had mentioned a television special about the paintings and artist. He always wanted his privacy. Maybe he is involved with Lynne now, and they will ride off in the sunset and leave us alone. That might be the answer.* Having conversations with myself had been my way of problem solving. I would think of all the possibilities and hoped one would materialize. Usually I had plan A or plan B and then oh, what the hell.

I called and kept the appointment that was pending. Dr. Sterling wasn't surprised. He explained that I had been fooling myself because I wanted so much to believe that Bryant was gone from my life. The first thing I had to admit to myself was that I still loved him, and I needed to determine why. That was no great revelation, I already knew that. Now tell me something I didn't know. He wasn't telling me how to solve the problem. I didn't come to him to remind me of my love for Bryant but to help me understand why it was there. At the end of our hour, I wasn't any further ahead than when I had walked into his office. With so much to do because the holidays were so close, this had been a waste of my time. Anger wasn't part of my personality, but I became angry with the doctor, Bryant, and mainly myself.

Dr. Sterling— sensing my hostility— tried to make me understand my anger. "You might think this session was a total loss, but I assure you it wasn't."

"Maybe the next time you can explain how much progress I made today, but I can't see it."

"You will. Be patient."

That was easy for him to say. He must have understood something

I didn't.

On the way home, I thought of what had to be done. I needed to tell Bryant to end this renewed friendship with Nick. He couldn't be part of our lives. Surely, Bryant knew that without my telling him. Or did he think I was completely over him? He walked away from me. Now he needs to find a life for himself and not share mine. Not even as a friend.

I had to keep my thoughts and fears from Nick. He had noticed my shortness lately. I knew he wondered when and if I would be seeing Dr. Sterling again. He had left the whole situation up to me asking no questions, and now it had begun to bother him. I had tried to convince him everything was fine. I got the impression that I wasn't fooling him.

I had planned an afternoon with Ann to finish up the shopping. Nick stayed with the baby and worked at home. That freed me completely for the entire day. Ann and I met for lunch. Shopping wasn't the only reason she wanted to meet. She had something to discuss with me.

She began by saying, "Before you say anything please hear me out. Nick called me. He is very worried about you. Please don't tell him I'm discussing this with you. I promised him I wouldn't. I share his concern. When we are talking on the phone, I get the feeling that you're not really with me. Several times I asked you a question and your answer was entirely out of context. What is the matter? Don't say 'nothing' because I know you too well. There is something troubling you. Is there something wrong between you and Nick? You're my best friend and I only want to help. Lately you have been moody, forgetful and miles away most of the time."

I sat there giving Ann my full attention. It seemed that was what she wanted. I became very defensive.

"You're right, Ann. Nick shouldn't have called you. It's none of your business."

I immediately regretted my outburst. "Oh Ann, I'm so sorry I said that. Please forgive me. You're right. Something is very wrong. I can't tell you. Please let me try to work this out by myself."

"Honey, you can't handle this by yourself. Don't you realize that?"

"Let's talk about this after the holidays. I just can't deal with it right now."

"Well, I hope it can wait that long."

"It will. I need to get the holidays behind me first. You know how much I enjoy them. I need to finish the shopping. That's my main priority today."

With that we dropped the subject and finished lunch. Then on to a full afternoon of shopping. I managed to get all the last minute gifts I needed.

As I turned into the driveway, I saw that we had company. I didn't recognize the car and assumed it was a client of Nick's. I opened the door and called out to Nick to help me with the packages. He came out to the car, opened the trunk, and jokingly gasped, "Is there anything left in the checking account?"

As we carried the packages into the house, Nick said, "Put your packages down and come into the living room. I have a surprise for you."

There standing by the fireplace was Bryant. I quickly excused myself telling Nick I must have eaten something that didn't agree with me at lunch, and that I really felt terrible. "Please give my apology to Bryant. I need to get to the bathroom immediately."

Nick excused himself and came up to me. So many emotions were consuming me, anger, fear, love, frustration, confusion and yes, even the longing to be near him one more time. I was trembling so I couldn't speak. Nick went back downstairs apologizing to Bryant that I was very ill and sorry the evening had to end like that. I knew I had to pull myself together before Nick returned. Bryant had asked Nick if there was anything he could do to help. Nick assured him that he could handle it and apologized for asking him to leave so abruptly.

"Nick, I understand. We'll get together at a more convenient time."

Nick returned as soon as Bryant had gone. "Let's get you into bed. Are you sure it was something you might have eaten? You really didn't feel too energetic this morning either. Do you think it might be the flu?"

"Maybe. I think I should sleep in the spare room tonight. I don't want you to get sick if it is the flu, and I don't want Victoria exposed."

"Don't worry. I'll take care of her tonight if she wakes up."

That was the first time we had not shared a bed since our wedding night. I was so exhausted all I wanted was to sleep. Nick wasn't next to me, and I wanted to be alone. That frightened me.

I spent most of the night trying to decide what needed to be done to end all this. Nick came into the room several times during the night. I pretended to be asleep. The next day I would call the doctor and reschedule as soon as the holidays were over.

I woke earlier than Nick and had breakfast ready for him. He was really surprised. I told him I felt great and that whatever it was, it was gone. He tried to believe me but I could see that he wasn't completely convinced.

Nick suggested that we cancel the Christmas party. I disagreed. The party was two days away and everything was almost ready. The caterers had begun to set things up in the dining room. I was looking forward to the party and nothing was going to spoil it. Nick decided it was what I needed to take my mind off whatever was troubling me.

Nick left for work. I called Dr. Sterling requesting something to help me relax and to make an appointment. Reluctantly he said he would phone in a prescription but only if I promised to keep the appointment.

The phone rang. I remembered that Bryant had said he would call. The caller ID had a number I wasn't familiar with so I assumed it was he. I didn't answer.

CHAPTER 17

The party was a success, and I was happy once again. Victoria was the hit of the party. Daddy had bought matching red velvet dresses trimmed with white lace and white satin roses for Victoria and me. He had surprised us with them the day of the party. He always knew the right thing to do or say to make my world right.

His face lit up brighter than the tree lights each time someone complimented him on the dresses. As they all told me how lucky I was to have such a thoughtful husband I had a hard time holding back the tears. Indeed I was surely blessed. I was sure God was looking down on me and saying, "I have given you a wonderful husband, a beautiful daughter, a great life with no hardships, and wonderful friends. I might have made a slight mistake on the special friend, but the rest turned out okay. So what is your problem, child?" He was right. The special friend, Bryant, was a mistake and mistakes can be rectified.

That evening I seemed much calmer. I found I didn't need to take the medication but I still needed to see the doctor. That hadn't changed.

Ann noticed that I was more like my old self. Once again I apologized for my previous rudeness during lunch the day we had gone shopping.

It was time for Santa to make his appearance. The children of our guests were ready and anxiously waiting. They were all wondering how Santa could come down the chimney since there was a fire in the fireplace. I explained that he only did that on Christmas Eve and would come through the door tonight. They all accepted that. Nick hired the perfect Santa since even I was convinced he really was Santa. Even his beard was real. The children all took turns sitting on his lap telling all they wanted. We sat Victoria on his lap and, of course, took lots of pictures.

When Santa left, the young lady next door entertained and served dinner to the children in the recreation room while the adults dined in the dining room. A few of the older children took turns holding and playing with Victoria.

After dinner Ann asked if she could get Victoria ready for bed. Watching them together I saw how much she meant to Ann. I began to appreciate how truly blessed I was. Ann was unable to have children and she accepted it. Even though she was really hurting inside each time she held a baby, she enjoyed every moment of it. She knew that no matter how much she wanted a child, it would never be. She filled her life with so much caring and giving to everyone whose life she touched. I returned to my guest and left her to rock Victoria to sleep.

When Ann returned to the living room for coffee and dessert, she was more radiant than I had ever seen her. She stood next to Stan and announced they had something to tell us. Puzzled, we all became very silent.

"I want all of our best friends to know that I am retiring in three weeks. Now I know that I am a little too young to retire, but we are going to become parents of a baby boy. After trying for a couple of years to adopt, we are finally getting a baby. It has really been difficult to keep this a secret for that past three months."

Little did she know that she was talking to the expert on secrets.

We all stood there for a moment and then began to give our congratulations. That was the most wonderful Christmas present she could have given me. We both cried, but this time they were tears of joy.

Now it was my turn to give a baby shower. The Christmas party soon became a baby shower planning party.

The party could not have been better, and it ended with me knowing what I now had to do. My family and friends needed the old me. The person they knew before Bryant entered my life. I also needed that girl back. This was the life I wanted not a life of uncertainty.

When the last guest had gone, Nick and I talked about the wonderful news and how glad we were that they had chosen that night to tell us about the baby.

The next day was Christmas Eve. The phone rang. It was Ann. She was crying. They were not going to become parents. The birth mother had decided to keep the baby. She stopped crying and with a very confident voice said, "I loved someone that wasn't mine to love, and now I must move on. Stan and I have each other and maybe in time there will be a baby in our future. Right now the pain is so great that we can't think about the future."

I told her we would be over as soon as Nick came home, but they wanted to be alone. Ann was right. They needed to have their private moments of sorrow.

We attended evening mass with Victoria. It is traditionally the children's mass, and they were all dressed in their holiday best. The children sang the carols with such enthusiasm. We looked at each other and knew that someday Victoria would be joining them and we would be proudly watching her.

On Christmas morning, we opened Victoria's gifts for her. She wasn't at all excited. All she really wanted was her bottle. Nick and I didn't exchange gifts that year. We decided to pick two needy families and give them the best Christmas possible. We bought all the gifts the children had put on their list and the food needed for the Christmas dinner. The children added a few things they wanted for their parents. Both families had invited us over, and we accepted. They wanted us to see what our gift meant to them. It was very rewarding. Another reason shown to me to be thankful for my life.

We then went to Ann and Stan's. We made the best of things, but it wasn't the day we had planned on. Ann showed us the nursery she decorated in anticipation of the arrival of their baby boy. All this had been planned in secret to completely surprise us. They wouldn't change it. Someday it would be used. We called it an early day and left for home.

In Ann's pain, I couldn't bring her into my problem. Dr. Sterling and I would solve it. She wouldn't understand now. When I have so much in my life, why would I want more? For example, Bryant in my life. She would think I was ungrateful. She would have been justified in thinking so. I could very well lose her friendship and that wasn't what I wanted. That would be a disaster for both of us.

CHAPTER 18

My appointment was scheduled before New Year's Eve. I wanted to start the New Year off with a resolution to resolve the problem.

The first question Dr. Sterling asked was how many pills I had taken to get me through Christmas. Proudly, I informed him I hadn't taken any. He was very surprised and wondered why I thought I needed them. I guessed I was stronger than I thought. He was pleased to hear that.

Now the big question. Was I ready to let go? I had tried so many times and failed. I told him what Ann had said when she found out the baby wasn't going to be hers. I put myself in that situation. Bryant was never mine to love. We had a very good session. I talked about all the good times we had had together. Then we came around to the same old fact that he didn't want what I wanted. He wanted me to be his friend because he truly cared about me, but he didn't love me. I couldn't accept that or understand why. When Nick came into my life and we got married, Bryant knew he could be my best friend now, and there could be no strings. He was safe, but he began to question his feelings.

I also realized that he wasn't trying to be part of my life. He did nothing to let me know about the exhibit. He was invited to our house by Nick, and should have refused, but he couldn't tell Nick why. Nick was the kind of person that people find hard to say no to. Bryant probably wanted to see my life now and know in his heart that he had made the right decision. I had the life and happiness he wished for me. The life he couldn't fit into or give me.

As I left the office I thought, *Wow, what progress today.* I was a long way from a solution, and I intended to continue the therapy. I felt a lot better about myself. For the first time in a long time, I was beginning to like myself again.

That night at dinner Nick asked, "Well, how did things go today? You seem to be a lot more like yourself. I sense a feeling of accomplishment. Am I right?"

"I guess you can say that. Things went really well today. I think things will be a lot better from now on. I know where I am going and what I have to do. I still need to work on the problem, but I think I'm closer to the answer now."

"Does this mean you are ready to share this with me?"

"Not quite yet."

"At least I didn't get a definite no. I've waited this long, a little longer won't hurt."

"It's a very personal problem and I can't say any more. All I need right now is your faith in me."

"You know you have that. The fact that you're getting professional help tells me that you are determined to take control of the problem."

All the while the thought that kept running through my mind was, *One more holiday for this year and a new year will begin. A new year and a new life.* As our guests started to arrive for our New Year's Eve party, I was very anxious to see Helen and Reggie. We had remained friends although Nick and I had given up boating and visiting the marina. We e-mailed at least twice a week. I had sent pictures of the baby's first Christmas.

When Helen and Reggie finally arrived, we didn't have a lot to catch up on thanks to e-mail. I noticed that Helen wasn't her usual perky self. I wanted to know what was troubling her. Nick and Reggie took the luggage to the spare room, leaving Helen and me to visit.

As soon as they were out of sight I said, "Okay Helen. What's wrong?"

Hesitating a moment, Helen told me that she had received a phone call from Nick. He was so worried about me that he had called and told her that I had a problem and was seeking professional help.

"He wanted to know if there was anything I could tell him that might help him understand and support you."

Nick was beyond concern. He was very troubled. He had confided in two of my best friends. "What did you tell him?"

118

"Only that I was sorry to hear about you, and I had no idea what was troubling you so."

Helen found it hard to tell me what she had to say next and struggled to find the words. "I know this isn't the time to bring this up, but I can't keep it to herself any longer. I was so upset with myself for telling Nick I had no idea what your problem was."

I was completely confused. Helen continued, "I know why you went to the island the day of the baby shower. I can't keep silent any longer."

I looked at her. Afraid to speak. "Helen, I don't understand. What are you trying to say?"

"I should have said something long before this, but I didn't know how. It happened that summer you had your miscarriage. Remember that night you were so upset and you wanted to be alone?"

"Yes, but that was a long time ago. What about it?"

"I came to see if I could help. When I got to your boat, you were gone. I saw you off in the distance walking towards the park. I went after you and saw you crying on the park bench. I waited a while and decided to stay in the background and make sure you would be all right. When you got up to leave, I saw that guy from the island walking towards you. I couldn't help but overhear your conversation. I know I should have walked away, but I didn't. You know the rest."

"Oh, Helen, why didn't you come to me the next day?"

"I didn't know what to say. I thought the two of you ended it that night. Then when you went to the island the day of your baby shower, I was surprised and wondered why. Since then I have been concerned about you and Nick. Does he know anything about this? Is that the problem between the two of you?"

"No, he doesn't, and I never want him to. I can never tell Nick the truth. It would destroy him and our life together. If I would have told him in the beginning, I could have convinced him how much I loved him, but now he can only wonder why I hid this from him. I'm so sorry you had to keep this secret for such a long time. I love Nick and we are a very happy family. Yes, that is over—well almost—I'm still working on it. Please don't mention this to anyone. I didn't know anyone knew about us. I need to explain everything to you, and I hope you will understand. Let's join the others, and I'll tell you the whole story later. I'm fine, so stop worrying. Does Reggie know?"

"No, I couldn't tell him. I really wanted to confide in him and get his opinion if I should tell you or not, but I decided not to."

"Thank you very much for that, Helen."

"You could have come to me if you had a problem. I imagined all sorts of things and was really hurt that you didn't. I was there for you when you lost Brian, and we have been through so much together."

"I didn't want anyone to know. Not even you."

Helen and Reggie were going to spend a few days with us, so I would have plenty of time to tell her everything. I was relieved that I had a friend to talk to. Dr. Sterling was helping, but sometimes a person needs a very close friend to confide in. I hadn't been able to do that. I knew Ann wouldn't understand or accept what I had done.

We joined the party and had a wonderful time. At the stroke of midnight, I truly knew it was going to be a great new year. Helen looked as if the world had been lifted off her shoulders. Ann and Stan were starting to get over their disappointment and looking forward to trying to adopt again. I was sure the new year was going to be a great one for all of us.

Ann and Stan were also spending the night, and Ann sensed that Helen and I needed to talk. Acknowledging the fact Helen and I didn't get to spend as much time together as she and I did, Ann excused herself and retired. I was sorry that I couldn't include her in this, but I knew I would lose her as a friend if she knew. I knew her well enough to be sure of that. There was no doubt in my mind.

After everyone had left, Helen and I had one last drink while the caterers cleaned up. It didn't take long until Helen and I were alone. I decided we would talk now if we weren't too tired. I started the whole story from the first day at the lighthouse up to the present. She just sat there saying nothing, just listening. At times I wondered what her thoughts were. She gasped as I told her about the incident at the art gallery, and that Nick and Bryant were old college friends.

When I had finished, she looked at me with tears in her eyes and said, "I should have come to you the next day and told you what I had seen. Maybe things would have been different if you knew you could tell me and trust me to keep your secret."

"No, it was my decision to keep the secret. That decision was wrong, and the past can't be changed. I know that the guilt of not telling Nick is one of the reasons I can't deal with this now."

"If I had…"

"Helen, there was nothing you could have done because I choose to keep our friendship a secret."

"Why?"

"I'm not quite sure now."

"Well, I'm here for you now. Please don't shut me out anymore."

I began to cry. "I'm fine as long as Bryant stays away. I need to let him know he must end his friendship with Nick. Nick is the one pursuing the friendship. I can't ask Nick to end a friendship he obviously wants. He wouldn't understand and I can't justify asking such a thing. Maybe it is time to tell him the truth."

Helen thought I should think things over and talk to Dr. Sterling before making a decision. She agreed that things seemed to be headed for a solution, but thought it was a little too soon and my sessions should continue until both the doctor and I came to the same conclusion. She was right. I didn't want to rush into that and find out that I had done something totally wrong. Something I might deeply regret.

We didn't realize how late it was and how much time had passed. The guys had gone to bed hours ago letting us stay up to visit. They knew we wanted to girl talk and thought it would be pretty boring for them. We finally called it a night. Helen said she would always be there for me no matter what time of day or night. I assured her that I would call if I really needed to talk.

The old year had ended on a very promising note and the New Year seemed to be starting out the same.

The next morning we wanted to sleep in, but Victoria— who had not ushered in the new year— was not in agreement. I got up and started for the nursery. Ann was already opening the nursery door. "Please let me take care of her this morning. I need this."

I could see tears of both happiness and sorrow in her eyes and said, "Of course, Helen and I stayed up quite late, and I could use a little more sleep."

Nick finally woke me. Breakfast would be on the table in ten minutes, and everyone was downstairs waiting for me. In fact, Helen was the first one up and had started breakfast. Ann had already fed Victoria. We all sat down and toasted the new morning with straight orange juice.

The next few days Helen and I didn't discuss the situation at all. Everything that needed to be said had been.

Helen, Reggie, Nick, Victoria and I had a wonderful time dining out, seeing the holiday lights around the city and spending quality time together. Helen and Reggie had never been to New York, and there was so much to show them. Ann was more than happy to take Victoria for an evening while Nick and I took Helen and Reggie to a Broadway show. In fact, it turned out to be Victoria's first sleep over at her godparent's home.

I really didn't want Helen and Reggie to leave, but the holidays were over, and they had to return home. I still felt bad that I couldn't share my problem with Ann since she was one of my best friends. I was content with just having Helen know. No one else needed to. My plan was for no one to ever know, but things don't always go according to plan. Boy, I would soon find that out.

CHAPTER 19

Several weeks had passed. I called Dr. Sterling. Hearing what had happened, he thought I had made a lot of progress, but sensed that I was not ready to tell Nick. We would talk about it at the next session.

The year started out with more snow than we needed. Victoria and I spent a lot of time in the house. I took her out when the weather was pleasant. Daddy had bought her a wooden sleigh. It looked like a miniature Santa sleigh. He had found it in a unique woodcraft shop. Daddy even took a few snow days to enjoy his daughter's new toy with her.

Just as I thought life couldn't be better and that complete happiness had once again come to me, Helen called.

"Catherine, I really didn't want to make this call, but you need to know. Bryant has been in an auto accident and might not make it. It seems that he was driving home and hit some black ice. He lost control of the car, and he hit a tree. No one else was involved. Most of the facts aren't clear yet. It was on the news just minutes ago. There was a suitcase in the backseat of the car. Whether he had been going on a trip or returning isn't clear as of yet. I don't know what you want to do, but I'm ready to support you on any decision you make."

It took a few seconds before I could talk. "Helen, he's only a friend now. I will always love him as a friend. I have to tell Nick the whole story, and let him decide what I should do."

"Catherine, are you ready for that? What if Nick doesn't understand? I really think he will, but only you can make that decision. I think Nick is the only one that can help you now."

"Well, I will have to take that chance. It is time for all our sakes. I know it is the only way I will have complete peace and happiness

123

in my marriage and with my family. I also need this to make the dreams stop forever. I have to put the past behind me or I will never rest."

When I hung up, I called Dr. Sterling to tell him what had happened, and that it was time to tell Nick. He wasn't too sure that the problem was clear enough in my own mind. Dr. Sterling would be there to help. I called Nick at work, and asked if he could take the afternoon off and meet me at the doctor's. He didn't ask questions, as usual, but relied on my judgement.

I called Ann to inquire if she was free the entire afternoon to stay with Victoria explaining I couldn't say any more at this time and to please trust me. Ann, as usual, was more than happy to spend the afternoon with her godchild.

"Catherine, I will always help in any way I can, but I must admit this secrecy of yours is beginning to really bug me. I hope you decide to tell me what is going on soon. My curiosity is working overtime. I'll be there as soon as possible."

Upon arriving and seeing Victoria, Ann forgot her impatience with me.

On my way to the doctor's office, I wondered whether my life as it was now, was ending. I knew I had to tell Nick, and I needed to go to Bryant. Not as a lover, but as a friend. I prayed Nick would understand.

When I got to Dr. Sterling's, Nick was waiting for me. I could see the look on his face was one of relief. He looked at me with those gentle eyes, as if to say it was about time I shared this with him and that he was ready help. His patience until now was unbelievable, and the time was now here. Now was definitely the time. There was no doubt in my mind, and I was convinced that I should have done this a long time ago.

Dr. Sterling introduced himself to Nick. He made us both feel comfortable and told me the floor was mine. He was there for moral support only. He had cancelled his afternoon sessions and would stay as long as it took.

I started the story from the beginning and didn't stop until the present moment. Nick just sat there listening. At times, I could see the hurt on his face. Then it would change to compassion, then an occasional smile, then confusion. But he didn't say a word. Three hours later, after hearing only the sound of my voice, I was finished. Dr. Sterling sat silently, as if it was Nick's turn first.

"This is something I didn't expect. I really don't know what to say. You know how much I love you. I don't understand why you felt you couldn't tell me. If you hadn't chosen me, I would not have given up as easily as Bryant did. I would have fought for your love. He will never know how much he gave up, and I will always be thankful to him for that. We can work all of this out together when you get back from Michigan."

"Do you honestly think I can handle seeing him again?"

"I want you to see him and come back to us. He may not have much time, and we have a lifetime. You may be the only true friend he has. You might be able to help him now. Remember he was there for you during difficult times."

We had almost forgotten that Dr. Sterling was sitting there. He cleared his throat and said, "Well, I guess you really didn't need moral support. I think the two of you have everything under control, but I am here if you need me."

We thanked him for all he had done for me in the past and assured him I would let him know how things turned out on my return. With that we left. On the way home, I followed behind Nick wondering what was going through his mind. I picked up my cell phone and called him.

"Are you all right? What are you thinking about at this moment?"

"I'm all right, and I'm thinking about you and what you must have gone through all this time. I wish I could have been there to help you. I would have seen you through anything as long as I knew you loved me. Now hang up and pay attention to the road. See you at home. I'm going to make your plane reservations now."

Ann met us at the door. Her expression was one of much concern and confusion. I had left without telling her why. I had to tell her something, but what?

"Ann, things have been going on in my life that I can't talk about to you at this time, but very soon I hope to tell you all about it."

"I know something has been bothering you for quite some time. Please let me know if I can help in any way."

Being a true friend, she left it at that. Assured that everything was fine and under control, she quietly said good-bye hugged and kissed us and left.

Nick called the office and told them he was taking a few weeks off for personal reasons.

I called Helen and gave her my itinerary. She said she would be at the airport to pick me up, but had no further news to convey.

CHAPTER 20

Due to my desire to get there hastily, the plane ride seemed to take longer than usual. I tried to think of what I would say if he could hear me. Even if he couldn't, I needed to let him know I was there. I knew he would feel my presence. I prayed I wouldn't be too late.

Helen was waiting for me. She was alone. As I got into the car I asked, "Does Reggie know?"

"I told you I wouldn't tell him unless you wanted me to."

"Thank you for that, Helen."

The hospital was a short twenty-minute drive from the airport. It seemed like hours. After Helen had told me that there was no further news about Bryant's condition, we drove in silence. I appreciated the fact that Helen let me have my space.

At the entrance to the hospital, Helen stopped the car, put her hand on mine, and asked if I wanted her to go in with me. Managing a smile, I thanked her and told her this was something I needed to do alone. She understood.

"Call me, and I'll pick you up regardless of the time."

"Thanks. I will. I want you to go home and tell Reggie everything now. He needs to know why I suddenly arrived in town without my family. No more secrets."

"Are you sure this is what you want?"

"Yes."

"I could check you into a hotel and no one would know you were in town."

"No. It's time to face my fears."

I walked up to the door and looked back. Helen hadn't pulled out of the driveway but sat there watching me in case I changed my mind and wanted her to accompany me. I questioned if I was ready to see him again, but I couldn't think about that any longer, I was here. They say time takes care of everything. Not this time.

I could feel my heart beating faster, and it seemed as though I was walking in slow motion. The front desk seemed so far away. I began to feel sick to my stomach, and my legs felt so weak that I thought I wouldn't make it to the desk. I knew I had to get control of my emotions. I reached the desk and as calmly as possible said, "I'm here to see Bryant Westover."

"He has a visitor. May I ask your name?"

"Tell him Catherine is here."

"Catherine?"

"Yes. I'm sure he will see me."

"When he was brought in he called out for someone named Catherine. Is that you?"

"Yes. I think so."

"We had no way of knowing who he was calling for because we had no last name to go by, and he was unable to say anything else. He isn't conscious. I'll get a nurse to take you to him in the intensive care unit."

Everything was happening so fast, I didn't have time to think now. I entered the room— and to my surprise— Lynne was sitting by his bed. She turned and looked at me with the same look she had given me at the island. She knew for whom he was calling and how to get in touch with me. She had chosen not to do that. She knew that Mae at the store and Helen knew me. Her surprise at seeing me was very evident.

In anger, Lynne said, "What are you doing here? Who called you?"

"That's not important now. I will tell you later, but now I need to be here by myself. I would appreciate it if you left us alone. The nurse told me he has been calling my name. You knew he was calling for me. So please, do as I ask."

She knew that her selfish act was keeping Bryant from the one person he wanted to have near him. She turned with tears running down her cheeks and began to cry.

"Now I know the secret he has been keeping and why he couldn't love me. It was you all the time standing between us."

"No. I wish I could tell you that you are right, but that is not his secret. I wish I knew, but I don't. Why he can't return love is his secret. Our friendship grew because I needed him at a very bad time in my life, and I never asked him to explain or discuss anything he didn't want to. We accepted each other for what we were."

"No. Catherine, you're wrong. He loves you very much even if he won't admit it. I tried to be part of his life, and he let me know that there could never be a future for us. The harder I tried, the more distant he became. I finally decided to take it one day at a time and hoped he might someday turn to me. It was better that way rather than not having him in my life at all."

With that she turned and walked out of the room. As she did, the nurse entered. She said he had been unconscious since shortly after the accident. I went up to him and gently reached for his hand. The nurse suggested I talk to him, and maybe there might be some sort of response evoked by the sound of my voice.

I leaned over him and gently kissed him on the forehead and then on his lips.

"It's my turn to be at your side as you were for me when I lost Brian. Even though you weren't there, I felt your presence when I thought I would lose Nick. Now I am here for you. Please hold on and fight."

I tried so hard to hold back the tears, but it was useless. As my tears fell on his face, I felt his finger move. I put my other hand on top of his and held on with both hands trying to give him some of my strength. I was remembering how we had always held hands while we were walking or just sitting on the beach talking. His strong, firm grip when I had a problem or a bad day had always comforted me. Now it was my turn. Time stood still as I sat there talking to him and reminding him of the days on the island. I thought we were still alone when I heard the nurse say, "Are you getting any response from him at all?"

"No, but it seemed as if he was trying to hold my hand. I could feel his fingers move a little so I held his hand tighter."

"Well, that is more of a response than any we have gotten. I hope you can stay with him and keep trying. Do you have to leave or can you stay?"

"I'm here just for him. I can stay as long as it takes if it will help, but I just flew in from New York, and I am pretty tired and hungry. Is there somewhere I can get something to eat?"

"I can call the cafeteria and see what they have and bring you something. What would you like?"

"A turkey sandwich. If they don't have that, a salad please, and coffee with cream."

While I waited for the nurse to return, I called Helen. She was starting to get worried. She said that it had been three hours since she had dropped me off. I apologized for not calling sooner. I hadn't realized how much time had gone by. I brought her up to date on how things were going, which wasn't good. I promised Helen I would keep her informed if there was a change in his condition. As I was telling her that I deeply cared for him as a friend only, the nurse had returned with my sandwich. I wondered how much she had overheard.

She placed the sandwich and the coffee on the table. I could see she was trying to decide what to say next, "I don't know what your plans are, but if you want to stay the night, we can bring in a lounge chair for you. It is really quite comfortable."

"Thank you very much. I'd like that in case I am getting through to him and he tries to respond. And if he does, I want to be here."

My next call was one I dreaded. My whole future was at stake. I wasn't sure how much I had hurt Nick, or if he really did understand. He had had time to think things through. Had he changed his mind? He had done exactly what I knew he would, making all the arrangements for me to leave and taking care of everything that needed to be done. Dialing the number, I began to tremble.

"Hi. I'm sorry to call so late."

"That's okay. I have been waiting for your call. How is Bryant?"

Hearing the sound of his voice eased my fears. "First, I miss you and Victoria very much already."

"We both miss you too. How was your flight?"

"Okay. No delays."

"I assume you are at the hospital."

"Yes, I am. I'm with Bryant right now." I wondered what he was thinking as I said those words.

"How is he?"

"He's unconscious. Things aren't going well here."

I told him everything that had happened from the time I left home and about the suggestion I stay in his room all night and why. He supported any decision I had to make. Why didn't that answer surprise me? I realized more each day how much I really was in love with my husband. When he asked if I was sure I was all right, I started to cry. I told him I didn't know what I had done to deserve him, and I wouldn't be able to bear it if I ever lost him.

"I love you very much and always will. Now dry your eyes and do what you feel needs to be done to help your friend. Remember, he's my friend also."

"I love you too. I'll be coming home as soon as I can. Kiss Victoria for me."

"I will. Goodnight. I'll be waiting for you to call again with better news."

For the first time since all of this had started, I had the feeling I could cope with anything and all would be resolved soon.

I called Helen, conveying my plan to stay the night and my conversation with Nick. She was relieved things were working out for us. She had explained the situation to Reggie, and he was quite shocked, but mainly by the fact that Helen had kept a secret from him.

"Helen, I can't face Reggie at this time."

"Catherine, true friends stand by each other, and Reggie feels as I do. We are true friends."

Those words of encouragement made things easier for me. I no longer had the fear of losing their friendship now that my friendship with Bryant was no long a secret.

I heard Reggie in the background, "Tell Catherine we're here for her and she should call if she needs us, no matter what time it is."

"I heard that, and thank you very much. I need to get back to

Bryant. Don't worry about me. Get some sleep. I'll keep in touch. Bye."

I returned to Bryant's side and took his hand. "Oh, I wish you would open your eyes and see I'm here for you." But he didn't. I moved the lounge chair next to the bed and closed my eyes. I drifted off to sleep immediately, still holding his hand.

I didn't know how long I had been sleeping. I don't know what woke me, the nurse opening the door or the sound of Bryant calling my name. Maybe I was dreaming. No. It wasn't a dream. He did say my name. The nurse rushed to his side. He opened his eyes and turned towards me. His eyes slowly closed again and tears were running down his cheeks. The nurse leaned over him and called his name.

"Bryant, can you hear me? Catherine is here."

There was no response.

"Let me try. Bryant it's me, Catherine. I'm here. Open your eyes. Please. Can you feel me holding your hand? Please try to open your eyes or squeeze my hand. Come on. We need to have one of our long talks. Remember the ones that lasted hours? I have so much to tell you, and I am sure you have lots to tell me."

I tried not to cry, but the tears came. As a tear dropped on his lips, weakly he said in his velvet voice, "Catherine," opened his eyes, and looked at me.

The nurse quickly asked me to move, and as I did, he motioned not to send me away. Explaining that I wasn't going anywhere, she sent for the doctor. I promised to stand where he could see me.

When the doctor and the nurses had finished all they had to do, I leaned over him and gave him a tender hug.

"You're too tired to talk now. Just rest. I'll be here when you wake up, I promise."

The doctor expressed his relief at seeing some sign of progress.

"Are you a relative?"

"No. I'm his friend Catherine."

"Your name was the only word he has spoken since being brought in. I don't know who got in touch with you, but I certainly am glad they did."

"A friend of mine called when she heard the news report on television."

"Do you know any next of kin we should get in touch with?"

"I regret saying I don't."

"I'll talk to you tomorrow about his injuries and prognosis. It is too early to know. He could slip back into the coma. We can't be sure of anything at this point. I hope you are the miracle he needed."

Everyone had gone and we were alone again. Bryant was very weak and pale. He managed a faint whisper, "Please" hesitating as if trying to catch his breath he said, "Stay."

He motioned for me to come closer. As I did, he whispered, " Need to tell you…time to share…"

"Don't worry about anything right now. You need to rest and whatever you have to say can wait. I have waited this long. A few more days won't matter."

With that he softly said, "Okay," and drifted off to sleep.

Maybe it was my imagination, but I thought I felt a slight grip of his hand as I held onto his. I looked at the clock and realized it was too late to call Nick or Helen. I would call them first thing in the morning after talking with the doctor. Bryant still wasn't out of the woods, but briefly regaining consciousness was a good sign.

I sat there for hours unable to sleep now. My body was there, but my heart and mind were in New York. The hour no longer seemed important. All I knew was I needed to hear Nick's voice. I reached for the phone. When Nick answered I said, "I'm sorry to call and wake you. I have no idea what time it is."

"That's fine honey. What's up?" Then the tone of his voice changed signaling he was wide-awake. "Is everything okay? Bryant's not…"

I quickly interrupted. "Oh, no. He briefly regained consciousness. I'm so sorry I called at such an hour and frightened you. I just miss you and Victoria so much I had to hear your voice. Let's not talk about Bryant right now. I'll tell you all about him after I talk to the doctor tomorrow. Right now all I want to hear about is you and our daughter. I was so afraid that since you've had time to think things over, you might have changed your mind on how you feel about all this. You will never know how sorry I am that I didn't tell you everything from the beginning."

"Honey, please let me talk now. First of all, it doesn't matter what time it is when you need to call. I'm glad things are a little better there. Most importantly, yes, I wish you would have told me, but you didn't. You had your reasons. Now none of that matters. Because of our love, we can work through anything and I really mean it. How are you dealing with the problem there?"

"I'm fine now that I have talked to you. I hope my being here helped Bryant briefly regain consciousness. The doctor said he we would talk to me in the morning. It's too soon for a diagnosis."

Nick listened as I told him all about Lynne and what had happened. He agreed that her motives should not have ruled her sense of responsibility for Bryant's health.

We talked for an hour when Nick abruptly said, "I hear Victoria. I had better go to her. Please try to get a little rest, Honey. I'll be waiting for you to call us tomorrow, or I should say later today. We both love and miss you. Good morning."

"I love and miss both of you. See you soon."

I can hardly remember putting the phone down. Was it complete exhaustion or relief that there would be no more secrets, dreams, or sleepless nights?

CHAPTER 21

Feeling a hand on my shoulder, I realized the nurse was gently trying to wake me. I was startled and jumped up. She apologized assuring me everything was fine. Bryant was awake and asking for me.

"I'm right here just catching a little sleep. You've had a nice long nap, and now it's my turn to catch a few winks."

I hoped he would see the humor in that and at least give me a little smile. He tried a faint one, but I could see what an effort it was. I told him, "Relax, I won't try to make you laugh."

The doctor entered the room and looked very pleased to see that Bryant was awake and feeling a little hungry. Then I knew he was on the way to recovery when he whispered, "Coffee...one cream...one sugar."

The nurse suggested I go down to the cafeteria and get some breakfast, and she would let me know when I could return. Bryant didn't want me to leave but I told him I would be right back. The doctor saw how upset he had gotten and recommended the nurse send down for breakfast for me.

"I think it best you not leave. Do you mind?"

"No, I'm not hungry anyway."

Bryant was sleeping again. The doctor turned to me and said, "Don't be too alarmed if he drifts in and out. He'll do that a lot. He is conscious, just tired and on a very strong pain medication."

He explained that Bryant had suffered head and extensive internal injuries. When he was brought in, he was bleeding internally. He was more concerned with the internal injuries rather than the head injuries. He felt he would make a full recovery, but it would be a long process.

Bryant slept most of the day, waking long enough to make sure I was still there. He tried to speak, but found it too difficult. I sat there all day talking and reading the newspaper to him. Anything that would let him hear the sound of my voice.

The nurse assured me Bryant would be sleeping for quite some time and told me to go home for a few hours' rest. If for any reason I would be needed sooner, they would call me. A hot shower sounded very good. Helen was more than eager to pick me up to learn the latest news. I wasn't sure I could face Reggie, but when he met us at the door he put his arms around me and said, "Friends never judge before listening to all the facts. Then they understand and give forgiveness when needed."

Sleep came before my head hit the pillow. When I finally woke the next morning, the sun was shining in a clear blue sky. It almost made one think it was a spring day, not a winter day of maybe fourteen degrees, if that warm.

Helen had breakfast ready, and we sat at the kitchen table enjoying the warmth of the sun shining through the window. I felt so relaxed and content for the first time in such a long time. I could have sat there all morning but I needed to get back to the hospital.

When I returned Bryant's door was slightly open. I could hear the doctor informing Bryant that there was the possibility of the injured leg never being able to heal completely. At that Bryant interrupted and said, "Don't tell Catherine."

"As you wish Bryant, but you won't be able to hide your condition forever."

I pushed the door open, pretending not to have heard a word. That seemed a little strange. I knew how private he had always been, but this didn't seem to be the time to conceal anything about his condition from me. I started to follow the doctor out of the room. Bryant had difficulty trying to talk, but he managed to say, "Don't." Since I didn't want to upset him, I sat down next to the bed.

Morning turned into afternoon, afternoon into evening and Bryant became more alert. I explained how long I had been there, adding that I was going to leave for the evening to have dinner with Helen and Reggie. As much as he wanted me to come back after dinner, he wanted me to stay at Helen's and get a good night's sleep if I promised to come back in the morning. I promised and gave him a kiss on the forehead.

As the days went on he became stronger. He asked about Nick and Victoria and wondered how I knew what had happened. I told him the whole story. From the beginning to telling Nick about our friendship until the present moment. Knowing Nick, he wasn't surprised that he had agreed to let me come to him. Needless to say, I did most of the talking. He just lay there and listened to me. Every so often he would ask a question or two. When he remarked that it was just like old times having long talks, I reminded him I was still doing most of the talking. We both laughed. Well, he attempted to laugh along with me. He said he could tell how happy I was now.

I wanted so to ask if he was happy and if there was someone special in his life, but it was obvious however, that he had not changed because he spoke of no one. I wondered if Lynne was part of his life, and if she had returned while I was gone. He didn't mention it, and neither did I. I decided not to tell him she had been there and what had happened the night I arrived. If they were working on a relationship, knowing she ignored his request may only damage any chance of a future together.

I talked to Nick at least three times a day. Bryant kept trying to tell me about whatever was haunting him, but I convinced him it could wait until he was much better. The only thing that mattered was his full recovery. I did wonder if and when he would tell me what the doctor tried to tell me that day, but he either forgot or chose not to discuss it.

After the first week, I went home for the weekend. Nick and Victoria picked me up at the airport. On the way home I had to ask the question I was afraid to; whose answer I feared.

"Are you really fine with this?"

"Yes I am, because your friendship had already developed before we met. I didn't have to try to influence, persuade or convince you that I was the right one for you. You decided that all on your own."

"It wasn't a hard decision to make. You always let me know how much you loved me in so many ways. We had the same dreams, and you made them all come true."

I glanced at Victoria. She had fallen asleep. It was so good to be home.

It was a wonderful weekend. Nick and I really worked on a playmate for Victoria. I was sure a beautiful new life had been created.

I didn't want to leave, but we knew I had to keep my promise. So, I left for Michigan, knowing I had finally ended the conflict I had had and now was concerned for a friend and only a friend.

CHAPTER 22

It was late afternoon when my plane arrived, and Helen and Reggie picked me up. We went out for dinner before going to the hospital. Nick and I had called Bryant daily while I was home so we knew he was doing better.

When I reached Bryant's room it was early evening, and I was so surprised to see him sitting up. His color was a little better, but it was obvious he was still in considerable pain. I walked over to him and gave him a kiss on the forehead. He looked at me and said, "I'm so glad you're back. I have a lot to explain to you."

"Are you sure you feel up to talking?"

"Yes. It's time. Let's start with the lighthouse. The reason you didn't find anything about it is because it isn't a real lighthouse. The cottage was the home my grandfather built for my grandmother. They lived on the island. My father was born on that island and in that cottage. At that time there was no lighthouse, just the cottage. They lived on the island during the summers and spent the winters at their home in Arizona.

"Well, when my grandmother was pregnant with my father, there had been a terrible storm. My grandfather knew that she was due any day. During the storm my grandmother went into labor. With forty mile an hour winds and eight-foot waves, it was impossible to get her to the mainland. My grandfather called the doctor and he said not to move her and he would be there as soon it was possible. Since she had a couple of weeks to go, the doctor hoped that the labor would stop. Shortly after the conversation with the doctor, the storm knocked down the phone line. By the time the storm ended, she was ready to deliver. She was in much pain and very weak. My grandfather realized something was very wrong with the way things were going. The storm lasted for two hours. When it ended, the doctor came to the island immediately. There were complications. He delivered the baby that night. My grandmother was too weak to be moved. She died a few days later. I never knew what went wrong because he would never talk about it with my father. I knew he blamed himself for being on the island and unable to get help sooner. He left the island and moved to the Chicago area. My great-grandparents were very wealthy, so my grandfather didn't have to worry about money. He invested what he had inherited and became even wealthier. My father was sent to private schools in Europe and didn't see much of his father. My grandfather threw himself into his work building an empire for my father.

"When my father was around five, my grandfather decided that they would spend their summers on the island. My father's childhood on the island was lonely, but he loved it there. Suddenly, a few years later without any explanation, they stopped going there.

"My grandfather never remarried or sold the island. Years later, when he had retired, he returned to the island. He had decided that it was time to sell it. But as he stepped on the island, he realized he felt so at home there and could feel my grandmother's presence. He had the cottage renovated and took care of the grounds himself. He remained there until he died, six years later. When my grandfather died, my father drifted away from the island, but never sold it. My grandfather had built a vast fortune, and my father followed in his footsteps as an investor."

I interrupted him during the story to ask questions, which he tried to answer to the best of his knowledge.

I looked at Bryant and saw he was really tiring but trying to continue his story. I didn't know what this had to do with me, but I was sure I would find out. His words became fainter, and he had to stop talking. It was becoming too difficult for him.

"Bryant, you need to rest now. Just sleep for a while and tell me the rest later. It's really late, and I'm pretty tired too. I'm going to call Helen to pick me up. We can continue this tomorrow."

"You're right. I'm so tired."

All the while he was telling me this story, he had held on to my hand. Now he let go and asked, "Will you give me a kiss before you leave?"

I looked at him and saw a very lonely, sad, confused man. This story obviously had something to do with why he was unable to love anyone. So I leaned over and gently kissed him on the lips and softly said good night. He closed his eyes and drifted off to sleep within minutes. I sat there a while longer. I gently slid my hand from his.

I had several things to take care of during the morning, so I didn't return to the hospital until after noon. As I walked into the room I saw that his bed was empty. My heart sank. I ran to the nurse's station and asked why he wasn't in his room. She assured me that Bryant was fine. They had just taken him down for x-rays. I returned to the room and couldn't hold back the tears. I had been so frightened that something had gone wrong. I knew he was still very ill. I thought all the talking the day before had taken its toll on him. I dried my eyes as he returned.

"Did you have a nice tour of the hospital halls today? I hope they haven't tired you out too much. Do you feel like company now?"

"I'm fine, and yes, I want you to stay. Where did I leave off yesterday?"

I brought him up to date. It took him a few minutes to collect his thoughts. I wondered how much of this story was going to be very painful for him to relive and if he was up to it. I began to realize it was something he had to do if he was ever to be free to love. He continued.

"The only thing my grandfather and father had in common was business. They never shared a life as father and son. He was always away at school or with a governess. Even on the island, there was a housekeeper to care for them. My father and grandfather had enjoyed sailing together.

"My father once told me that if he had never been born, my grandmother wouldn't have died. He felt that my grandfather had never forgiven him for living and her dying. The bedroom she died in at the cottage was locked and he was the only one allowed to enter it. The home in Arizona was closed and left just as they had left it that last winter. He never got over her death. The home in Scotland was sold. He did keep the one in France.

"Grandfather had been living on the island for the last six years and in bad health. One day he called and asked my father to come to him. He needed to talk. My father was surprised that he wanted them to spend the remaining days of his life together. The next two months my grandfather tried to mend all those years. He told him he really did love him but was afraid to show it because he was afraid of losing him. He had loved my grandmother so deeply that life without her had no meaning. He was sorry and realized too late that he had been wrong for so many years. My father looked very much like his mother, the blond hair, the soft blue eyes and the smile that melted your heart. Every time my grandfather looked at my father, he saw my grandmother. Then he would think about how life would have been if she had lived and became angry. Later he realized that the greatest gift of love she had given him was their son. He began to regret how he had spent his life, but it was too late. Now all he could do was hope for forgiveness. He shared all the things my father had never known about his mother. At last there were stories to go with all the pictures of her. The locked room was opened, and so was my grandfather's heart. After grandfather died, my father never locked that door again.

"My father returned to Europe where he had spent so much of his life in schools there. Most of his friends were there also. Dad lived in the family home in France for the next year. He met my mother there. She was an American studying art. It was love at first sight and a whirlwind romance. They fell in love, got married and returned to America. My mother was a talented artist.

"The first year of their marriage, they traveled all over Michigan visiting lighthouses. She loved painting them. They spent a summer on the island and decided to make their home there. She asked my father to build a lighthouse next to the house. He thought she was crazy to ask such a thing, but he loved her so much that he would do anything she asked. That is why the lighthouse isn't tall enough to be a real lighthouse. The very top was her studio."

"I understand now why it isn't visible from the river. It would have confused the boaters."

"Right, and the trees hide it quite well. While the lighthouse was being built, my parents decided it was time to start a family. At first she was happy with the thought of becoming a mother. Then for no apparent reason, she decided she wasn't ready. She said she wanted to move to Paris for a short time. Those plans soon changed. She was pregnant. After I was born, she stopped thinking about Paris. She was happy with having a son and her painting.

"I remember sitting by my mom's side while she painted. She would make up stories to go with each lighthouse. I don't remember much, but I do remember her love for art. We spent each summer on the island, just like my grandparents had, and then went back to the old homestead in Arizona for the winter. The walls of the lighthouse were lined with her paintings from the bottom floor up the winding stairs to the studio at the top."

I interrupted him many times asking questions. He remarked that I hadn't changed a bit, still asking a million questions.

"For the next eight years, my mom seemed very happy. But then she became restless and asked my father if she could return to Europe to study further. He tried to convince her there were very good schools in America, but she disagreed. Reluctantly, he agreed to let her go. She said she would get settled, and we could join her. A few weeks later she called from Paris with the news that she wasn't returning to school after all. She had decided to travel around Europe and paint. My father was upset with that and said we would join her immediately. She refused to let us join her claiming she needed to be alone to paint for a short time. Dad and I were on the next plane to France. By the time we arrived at our home in Paris, she was gone. She hadn't gotten in touch with any of their friends or acquaintances, so they were unaware she had been there. We stayed there for two months waiting for her to return. During that time, my dad went everywhere he thought she might have gone. There wasn't a trace of her. It was as if she had ceased to exist.

"I remembered my father finding a few sketches in the apartment.

She seemed to have changed her interest from lighthouses to cathedrals. As he studied them closely, he recognized the area. It was the Basilica of Sacre-Coeur in Montmartre. Of course that was where she would go. The streets were lined with aspiring artists and hundreds of paintings. He was sure someone there would know her. Maybe she was still there. He made me believe that she was traveling around and would come back. In the meantime, we would also see the sights. What a wonderful vacation it was for us. But when we got to Montmartre, she had left. Several artists remembered her and that she painted lighthouses and cathedrals. Eventually we found a woman who knew my mother and told us where she lived. My dad's face lit up for the first time since we had left the United States. When we reached the house the landlady said my mother had paid for two months, but left in three weeks without leaving a forwarding address. The landlady said she had left a few sketches behind that might be of some help to him. The lady gave them to my father. One was of Notre-Dame. The others were crude attempts of something that looked familiar, but my dad couldn't quite recognize the places. We took them back to our apartment. My father sat for hours trying to remember where he had seen them or something like them. He kept studying the sketches and suddenly mumbled somewhat questionably, 'High Altar of the Shrine of the Three Magi?' I didn't know what that meant, and then he calmly announced we were going to visit Germany. That was so great, Dad and I traveling again. The next morning we packed and set off for Germany. I later learned that the 'High Altar of the Shrine of the Three Magi' was part of the Cathedral of Koln. Another dead-end. As much as I loved all the traveling and the cathedrals, I had seen enough of them. I wanted to see something of interest to a kid. I had the feeling this wouldn't be that kind of a trip and I was right. Seeing my dad hurting more each day with each disappointment, I went silently along and made him believe it was the perfect vacation. Each time he heard that there would be a gathering of artists selling their paintings, off we would go. At the Centrum in Leuven, Belgium, there were several paintings that might have been hers. After questioning the artist, we found she had left them with him to sell in payment of a loan he had made to her. He thought she had moved on to a showing at the Centrum in Burgee, Belgium."

Listening to that velvet voice, which was a little softer now, he made me feel as if I was walking down the streets in each city next to him. I had to change the subject.

"Wow. Look at the time. I can't believe we've been talking all day. I need to call Nick. Would you like to talk to him?"

"Not right now. I've talked too much today. My throat seems pretty dry and a little sore. You can leave and go back to Helen's where you can have a nice chat with Nick without any interruptions. He needs to hear your voice, not mine."

"I shouldn't have worn you out so. Tomorrow the doctor is going to consider letting you go home within the next few days, so I will be back in the morning to talk to him. If you want, I will stay with you until you find a housekeeper. Anyway, I need to hear the rest of this story. You know you have been keeping me captive with your saga. Who knows, I might write a book about your life."

I leaned over him and kissed him good night on the forehead. He thanked me again for being there, and for my patience.

CHAPTER 23

I drove to Helen's with more of an understanding of Bryant than I had ever had. Thinking ahead, I had the feeling that their search was never going to end and Bryant's mother would never be found. That plus the sad tale of his grandparents would have certainly shaped his life and emotions.

I called Nick as soon as I got to Helen's and gave him a shorter version of all that Bryant had told me. Hearing the news that Bryant might be going home soon, Nick had a surprise for me also. Victoria and he were coming to Michigan on the weekend for a few days. Nick had arranged everything with the help of Helen. She promised to keep it a secret until he could tell me himself. He wanted Bryant to hold the rest of the story until he arrived.

The next day was a busy one with talking to the doctor, and making arrangements for physical therapy sessions for Bryant after his release from the hospital. His leg had been badly crushed.

Bryant had rented an apartment on the mainland for the winter. That was were he had been living before the accident. He gave me the key so I could get the apartment ready for his return. I gave him the good news about Nick and Victoria's forthcoming visit.

"Nick wants to hear the rest of your story."

"You told him? Why? I've never told anyone but you."

"I'm sorry. I've upset you. I didn't think you would mind. He was your friend before you were mine. He is just as concerned about you as I. When I told Nick about our friendship, I promised myself that I would share everything about us with him from now on."

"No. I'm sorry for reacting the way I did. You're right. He is your husband and he could have refused to let you come here when I needed you. I've been alone and bitter for so long. Telling you all this has made me understand myself. Thank you. Now give me a kiss before you leave. One on the cheek will be fine."

Was he trying to imagine how it felt having his mother kiss him gently on the cheek and forehead before tucking him in for the night? Something I am sure he hadn't experienced from early on in his childhood.

During the next two days, I spent more time arranging for Nick and Victoria's visit, and getting Bryant's apartment ready for him than I had spent at the hospital. Knowing he was almost ready to go home, I didn't feel guilty.

I had rented a car because I didn't want to impose on Helen any more than I had to. On the day of my family's arrival, I drove to the airport as if on a cloud. This was Victoria's first visit to Michigan. It was my first time here during the winter, and the scenery was beautiful. We had snow in New York, but it seemed so different here. The fields along side the roadways were covered with untouched snow. It was like a beautiful white blanket had been thrown from the sky and covered the entire countryside. As the sunbeams hit the snow, it sparkled as if millions of diamonds were scattered on top. The sight brought back the memory of the painting of the blanket on the snow and Bryant's explanation of what he was saying.

The plane was on time, and I was waiting for my family as they came through the walkway. I couldn't wait to see Victoria's face when she heard my voice. Wouldn't you know it, she was fast asleep in her father's arms. He handed her to me and took us in his arms holding on tightly.

"It feels so good to hold Victoria again and have your arms around me. I have good news for you. Bryant will be going home within the next couple of days, and I will be going back home with you."

"That sounds wonderful to me. Is Bryant doing that well?"

"He needs more surgery on his leg. Hopefully he will regain full use of it. I've been as useful as I could be, and now it's time for Bryant to move on and find himself."

"And it looks as if you have found yourself."

"Did I wait too long to find myself?"

"I can't tell you this hasn't affected me at all, because it has.

Everything happened so fast. I was in total shock. At first, when you left, I was so hurt, I wasn't sure I wanted you to return, but as the days went on and you weren't there, I realized how empty my life would be without you. Our marriage was worth saving and there was Victoria to think about too."

"But when I called, I had no idea you felt this way. You told me everything was okay. Why didn't you tell me how you really felt?"

"You had enough on your mind and had made so much progress with the doctor, I didn't want to set you back to where you were months ago. We will work this out together."

"Yes we will, but first I must finish my obligation here."

We agreed to continue sessions with Dr. Sterling together when we returned home.

We took Victoria to Helen's and went to the hospital. Bryant was really glad to see us but disappointed that we hadn't brought the baby. During the whole time I had known him, I had never heard him talk about children or wanting them around. So I was surprised to hear this. In fact, when I had tried to talk about my class and the cute things the children would do, he had quickly changed the subject. I had begun to understand why, and so much more.

Seeing that Bryant was much stronger physically these last few days, I suggested that I leave the guys alone for a while to visit. Bryant said, "No, don't go yet. I have some really good news. I am going home tomorrow if everything is ready for me. I really want us to spend some time together, and I want both of you to hear the rest of my story."

Nick and I were very glad to hear the news.

"Well, in that case, I must really leave the two of you alone and make sure everything is ready for you. I've done some grocery shopping for you, but I didn't want to get the perishables until I knew when you would be going home. Do you think you can manage to fix a few meals for yourself when you get home, or do you want me to hire someone to be there a few hours a day?"

"I think I'll be able to do that for myself. After all, I'm used to cooking, but I would like for you to find someone to come in and do the housework for a month or so."

This time as I left Bryant's room, I turned to Nick and kissed him goodbye. Bryant and I waved goodbye to each other.

Walking to the car, I began to wonder if it was a good idea to leave them alone. I didn't know if they would discuss our 'love' triangle or let it go, but I had to let them sort this out for themselves. Whatever their decision, I had to let them resolve their relationship without my influence or presence. If they chose to discuss this with my being present, they would let me know. I prayed they wouldn't. Either way, the suspense was killing me, but I left quietly and went to take care of the matters at hand, getting ready for Bryant's release from the hospital.

I went straight to Helen's because I knew she would know someone that could help Bryant a few hours a day. We could stay in Michigan until he was settled and found someone, but we would return home together. I felt my duty to him was over and so was his hold on me. But I really did want to hear the rest of his story. So far it had really given me a new outlook on his feelings and fears. *Face your fears, respect and learn from them. I think he is beginning to do that.* As all those thoughts raced through my mind, I realized Helen was talking to me.

"Catherine, are you with me? You seem a million miles away."

"I'm sorry. Yes part of me is here and part is in the past. I'll explain later, but go on."

"I know a couple of women who could help Bryant when he gets home. Do you want to talk to them yourself? I could give you their phone numbers, or I could call for you."

"That's fine. Just call them and I'll let you decide who qualifies. You know the situation as well as I do since I've told you all there is to know about him."

"Catherine, you know that girl that was doing some work at the house while he was renovating might just be the right person. I heard that he had been seen with her a few times at the coffee shop."

"You didn't tell me anything about that. Why not?"

"I only heard about it a few days ago while I was talking to Mae

149

at the grocery store. Why? Does it make a difference?"

"No, not really. Go ahead and take care of it. I will be gone in a few days anyway, and the problem will be hers not mine."

"What do you mean 'problem'? Catherine, what on earth is going on with you? You seem so on edge. What happened at the hospital?"

"Helen, I'm not sure I should have left Nick and Bryant alone. I'm afraid of what they are talking about. I know how I feel, but I'm not sure about Bryant."

"What difference does it make how he feels? Come on, Catherine, please don't tell me you are beginning to have doubts again. My heaven girl, look at what you have here. Don't throw it away for something that can never be."

"Oh, no. Helen you have it wrong."

"Well, then tell me what you are talking about, and convince me I'm wrong."

I hadn't revealed to Helen the incident with Lynne that first night at the hospital. So I told her what had happened.

"Helen, I don't know why she was there. I should have listened to her and not judge her so quickly. How strong is their relationship? What did he tell her if anything about me? That's why I'm not sure if you should ask her to do this."

I told Helen it was time I talked to Lynne, and she agreed with a sigh of relief. Maybe Lynne was the right one to ask for help, but I would have to let Bryant make that final decision. That might answer a few questions I won't have to ask.

I had stayed away from the hospital the entire day to give the guys all the time they needed. Helen and I took the baby and went visiting. All our friends were so glad to see us. Since no one knew that I had been in town prior to this visit, I only had to tell them that Nick and Bryant were old college friends and had run into each other in New York where they had become reacquainted. They were satisfied with that and asked no questions. Seeing the baby was all they were really interested in anyway. Not that they weren't glad to see me. They knew I understood. Helen called a few of our close friends and invited them to join us at dinner so everyone could see

Nick. That sounded great to me.

I called the hospital room and told Nick our plans for dinner. Bryant was a little tired, and Nick was ready to leave, so I picked him up at the front entrance. I needed to know what if anything had been discussed. Nick knew by the look on my face what was on my mind even though I tried not to show my anxiety. He smiled, gave me a kiss and said, "Catherine, if you think there were no women in my life before you, you're wrong. I had female friends that were special to me too. I hadn't gone through what you had losing someone who was my whole life. I didn't need a very special friend to help me through a very rough time. If I had, I would have wanted it to be you. You were looking for something you had lost, and Bryant was looking for something he never had, or at least he thought he hadn't. Everything is fine. We will be better than ever now. I'm only sorry you didn't share this with me sooner. I would have been able to stop the pain and the dreams. I wish you could have helped Bryant, but I don't think anyone can until he finds himself. Now give me a big smile and a kiss, and let's join our friends at dinner. I'm starved. That hospital coffee and food is not my idea of food or drink. I need a good margarita."

Nick didn't tell me what he and Bryant had talked about, and I didn't ask. He had said it all, and there was no need to say anything else. With tears in my eyes, I gave him a kiss he would never forget, sat back, and said that would have to hold him through dinner. I promised to deliver a special evening after dinner. With a flirting grin he said, "I can't wait to see what you mean."

That evening at dinner we all had a wonderful time laughing and reminiscing about the guys teaching this city guy how to fish. There were a few new stories I hadn't heard, and I knew why. Nick blushed and then laughingly reminded them of their promise never to tell those stories. Since Helen's niece was watching the baby, we didn't rush through dinner, but sat there for a couple of hours having fun and remembering the good time we had spent together.

What a wonderful day and evening we had had. When we got into bed Nick reminded me that the kiss earlier was to last through dinner. Dinner was over now and he wondered what I had in mind for him. Needless to say, he wasn't disappointed. I was sure our lovemaking would take up the better part of the rest of the evening.

CHAPTER 24

Morning came and with it reality. I didn't know how I would approach Lynne or if I even could, but I had to try. Agreeing to see me, she invited me to her home. She greeted me with a puzzled look on her face. The first thing I had to let her know was that I was sorry I had acted as I did in the hospital, and that I should have given her a chance to tell her side of the story.

Leaving out the fact that I had learned she had been seen with Bryant several times off the island, I explained that since I knew how concerned she had been about Bryant I thought she might be able to help him when he was released from the hospital. I did tell her I figured they must be pretty good friends because she was the one by his side when I arrived at the hospital. No one else had even come to visit him. She told me that Bryant had called her several times when I had gone back to New York and asked her to visit him. Something he didn't mentioned to me, but he didn't have to. He didn't have to tell me anything about his life he didn't feel needed to be said.

She said, "Did you clear this with Bryant?"

"No, not yet. I wanted to ask you first. I didn't want to suggest it and then have you refuse."

"If it's okay with Bryant, I'd be glad to help him. I can take some time away from the shop. Just what did you have in mind as far as help?"

"He'll need someone to help with the housework until he is able to get around on his own. He'll be in a wheelchair for a few weeks or longer. He needs to be taken to physical therapy at least twice a week for a while. I really can't say how long he will need you or want someone around. That will be up to him to decide."

"Catherine, I will do this because you must know, I love him very much. I also know that he loves you even though he doesn't realize it or is in denial. I'll keep trying to make him forget you, and I'll be there when he does."

She needed to know how things were now. "If it helps you to make up your mind, he knows how much I love my husband. I did love him once very much, but he didn't return my love at that time when I really needed it. When I met Nick I had a decision to make, and I have never regretted choosing Nick to fulfill my dreams and my life. Bryant again came into our lives by accident. He had gone to college with my husband. So Nick was the one that renewed their friendship."

Lynne interrupted by saying, "Yes I know all about that. The first time he called asking me to come to the hospital, I almost refused, but I couldn't. I knew it was only because you had gone home. All I knew was I had to be with him. He told me about meeting the two of you at the art gallery. I thought you were out of his life, but fate brought you back into his life. He told me about you and that your husband was an old college friend. He said he knew you before your marriage. I still don't know how you met, and maybe I don't want to. If Bryant agrees, I will help all I can."

"I'll get back with you as soon as I let Bryant know we have spoken, and I'm sure he'll agree to hire you."

"Hire me? No, I want him to know I am doing this as a friend helping a friend. I hope he will see things differently in the future."

"I think that is something the two of you need to work out together. Bryant will be getting in touch with you."

I hoped I wasn't doing the wrong thing, but I felt I wasn't. Lynne stood at the door as I left. I was sure she was hoping this would be the last time she would see me.

I went directly to the hospital and told Bryant about my visit with Lynne, leaving out most of the details of our conversation. He was curious about why I had asked her. I finally told him that she was at the hospital at his bedside the night I arrived. That was as far as I went about that night. He didn't need to know any more unless she decided to tell him someday. That look of non-concern came over his face, and I wasn't sure what he was thinking. He didn't refuse Lynne's help. However, he had a request.

"I'm being released tomorrow, and if you don't mind, I would like you to pick me up. Is that all right with you?"

"Of course it is. Remember, you have a story to finish. A story Nick and I are very anxious to hear."

I left the hospital knowing that I had made the right decision again. Bryant assured me he would call Lynne and set up the arrangements. I needed to get out of his life and stay out if she was to have any chance at all.

That evening Lynne called and said, "I want to thank you for what you are trying to do. I really misjudged you also."

"We've both made mistakes, Lynne. I'm glad we can forgive each other."

We said our good-byes, knowing we could never be friends because that would keep me in Bryant's life.

CHAPTER 25

The hospital called the next day. Bryant had been released. I brought the car around, and Nick went inside to get him. As Bryant got into the car he asked, "Where's Victoria? I thought you were bringing her along."

As Nick helped Bryant into the car he said, "It's her nap time, and we thought you didn't need a baby around on your first day home."

"I was looking forward to seeing her."

Surprised again that he wanted to see Victoria, I came up with a plan.

"When we get you settled in, Nick will go back to Helen's to get her while I make dinner for all of us. How does that sound? Okay with you, Nick?"

"Sure, that sounds good to me."

Nick helped Bryant into the apartment. He said he would be back shortly with Victoria. Bryant was still pretty weak. He said he could use a nap while I prepared dinner. I was glad. I felt uncomfortable being alone with him because I wasn't sure Nick was comfortable with the idea. Nick and Victoria arrived an hour later.

After dinner we took Victoria back to Helen's and returned with a good bottle of wine. Bryant wanted to continue and finish his story before we left for home.

Bryant's apartment was cozy and well decorated. I wondered if he had rented it that way or if Lynne had decorated it, but I didn't ask. Nick started a fire in the fireplace, and we opened the wine. We all settled down as if we were going to watch the best movie of the year. Bryant remarked that all we needed was popcorn, but that it didn't go well with wine. "Well, cheese and crackers do go with wine, and I just happen to have picked some up at the store today." I chimed in cheerily.

Bryant knew exactly where he had stopped his story.

"Well to begin where I left off. Each summer for the next two years, my father and I traveled all over Europe searching for my mother. I began to wonder if he was searching out of love or anger. My father was a very proud man, and I knew he couldn't return home without knowing why she had left him. After each trip, everyone expected him to bring his wife back with him. He had let everyone believe that they were still together and she preferred to live in France for a while longer to paint. Summer vacation was coming to an end, and we were forced to return home. I would be sent off to a private school. I resented that. I wanted to stay with him. Much to my surprise my father agreed. I entered public school for the first time at the age of twelve. As for what he told his friends about my mother, I never knew. It was a closed subject. I couldn't figure out if he was a man deeply in love or just angry. A little of both I suspected. He then told me that Elizabeth, that was my mother's name, would never return. From that time on, he never referred to her as 'your mother', but as 'Elizabeth'.

"I didn't believe that she would never return. I knew that he never stopped looking for her. I figured out that most of his business trips were actually his following leads he had gotten on her possible location. We went to California and stayed at Malibu going to each art show along Venice Beach one entire summer. I only wished my father could have enjoyed all that traveling as I had.

"When I was fourteen, my father decided to return to the lighthouse for a summer. That came as quite a surprised since we hadn't been there in years. My father had spoken so much in the early days about the island I began to wonder if the memories were his or mine.

"The day we arrived he sent me to my room to unpack. Our housekeeper had always done that for me. I thought he had decided it was time I started being more independent. While I was in my room unpacking, he closed my door. I heard a lock click and a door being closed. Then banging and crashing sounds could be heard as if things were being thrown against a wall. The noise was coming from the lighthouse section of the house. When the noise had stopped, my father came to my room and told me the door to the lighthouse was locked and should never be opened again. I knew my mother's paintings were on the wall from the bottom step to the very top and he had destroyed them. The thought made me ill. It was all I had of her. We only stayed a week, and he became unbearable. Destroying the paintings only made him angrier. I was glad to leave the island.

"For years after that I thought he had sold the island. He said it was no longer a part of our lives. As time passed, I couldn't picture my mother's face at all. Every picture of her had been removed from our home. He sold the home in France.

"He had finally given up. From that day at the island, until his death, I never heard him mention her name again. It was as if she never existed, but she did to me. I never stopped wondering why she had left and wishing that she would return.

"We then moved to Chicago, and that was where we stayed. Like my grandfather, my father buried himself in his work. We took vacations, but they usually involved a business trip also. We never left the country again. He would send someone else if the trip involved the European associates.

"When I was about fifteen, the housekeeper once said something about the mail I had been receiving from France. I didn't think much about it because my father told me they were letters from a private school wanting me to consider them. I didn't ask questions because I didn't want to go to school in Europe. We had become very close, and I knew how much he needed and loved me. I trusted him to do what was right for me. I tried so hard to do whatever it took to please him. Unlike his father, he didn't turn away from me. Instead I became his whole life. Sometimes I felt he was a little over-protective.

"History does have a way of repeating itself. Nick, remember when I suddenly left college that year? It was because my father had suffered a near-fatal heart attack. It left him completely incapacitated. I was told he wouldn't last six months and stayed with him till the end. I owed him that much. I never told him of my ambition to become an artist, knowing it would hurt him too much. I painted a little in college, as you know Nick, hiding my work when he would visit.

"After he died, I was going through his personal things in his desk and the safe in his study and found the deed to the island and lighthouse. He hadn't sold it, and I wondered why he made me believe that he had. I was once again surprised with the names on the deed. It read, 'Jerome Westmore and Bryant Westmore, with rights to survivor.' He had put my name on the deed without telling me. Wrapped up with the deed was a key. I had no idea at first what the key meant. Then I remembered. After he had destroyed the paintings he had locked the door. I knew he had never gone back because we were always together. On the other hand, he could have gone back without my knowing once I had gone away to college.

"The Westmore estate was a big responsibility for me; one I handled poorly. I didn't take too much interest in the family fortune. Unfortunately all I did was spend it. I soon realized that I had better get involved in preserving it. With the help of Dad's attorneys and associates, I became quite a businessman, but we won't go into that part of my life now.

"Years after I had taken care of his affairs, I decided to take a look at my island. I didn't know how I would feel or if I would want to return, but I felt the need to find out. When I opened the door, everything was as we had left it. The first thing I had to do was to unlock the door. My grandfather had locked a door that my father opened, so my father locked a door that I now must open.

"I looked in horror at the beautiful paintings that lay slashed and destroyed at the foot of the stairs. Each one had been slashed beyond repair. I visited the island over the next four years without anyone knowing. While I was there, I studied each picture and painted it again. They were her ideas and paintings reproduced by me. I wanted so much to be a successful artist and now that my father was gone, my dream could be a reality without hurting him. I had inherited a vast fortune. I put up all the money for the showing in New York that you saw. When I realized how successful it was and that I could have sold every painting, I had to close the show. Those paintings weren't mine. They were my mother's copied by me. No one would ever know, but I did. I even thought what if she would somehow learn about the exhibit and see what I had done. She would have known they were hers. That was what I really wanted to happen, and why I showed the paintings. Unlike my father, I never gave up hope that she would return, even though it was never mentioned.

"You know the rest of the story. Catherine found me here. I often wonder if I would have remained a recluse if she hadn't been so persistent. By trying to help her, I began to realize how much I was missing in my life. So many times I had come close to finding my mother, and I'm still looking. The night of the accident I was on my way to the airport to follow a lead. As more time passes, the leads grow further apart. My fear is that someday they will completely cease. Maybe that would be the best ending, and I could let go and move on. I need to know why she didn't love me enough to return or even try to reach me."

Nick and I sat there not knowing what to say. I knew what it was like to lose someone you loved so much and wonder why. Each person must search and find the answer for him or herself. My answer came with the help of Bryant and through meeting Nick, but not everyone is as lucky as I was. Sometimes I still wonder why Brian had died, but I knew that in looking for an answer I had found love again. Bryant had been searching for an answer but refused to let anyone into his life that would open his heart to love. He needed to put closure to mother's disappearance before he could ever love anyone. Bryant knew that his father had never stopped loving his mother even though he denied it till his death.

Nick asked if there was anything we could do. Bryant tried to remember the lead he was following, but he couldn't. He had seen something on television and was rushing to the airport to catch the first plane to Paris, France, and that was the only thing he had remembered.

"I often wondered about the letters I had received from the private school in Europe. I never asked my father why they kept sending them to me. I had never seen them or knew what he had done with them. Once he threw one in the fireplace and stood there until it completely burned staring at the fire and said he wished she would leave us alone. I asked who she was and he said, 'You misunderstood me. I said 'they' not 'she'. There were times when I thought maybe the letters were from my mother, but I felt he would never have ignored any word from her because he still loved her deeply. I felt it was wishful thinking on my part. What a cruel joke life played on me that night I crashed. I had the feeling this was going to be my final search. I would be able to move on with my life."

As Bryant uttered those words, I remembered thinking life had played a cruel joke on me when Brian died. We had had so many dreams and plans, and then they were gone. He had just longings, no dreams, no plans, and no past with his mother in it.

The hour was late, and Bryant suggested that Nick and I spend the night in the guestroom. To my surprise it didn't bother me. It was obviously a very natural suggestion made by a concerned friend. Nick thanked him but said we needed to get back to Helen's because of the baby.

Nick wanted to get a listing of all the programs on television before the night of the accident. Maybe something would jolt Bryant's memory. That was a project for Nick and Bryant. I planned on spending the extra time with friends. With those plans made, Nick and I left and returned to Helen's.

CHAPTER 26

The next morning I knew that Lynne would be going to Bryant's, and she didn't need me in her way. She really loved him. I think he knew that too.

That afternoon my mind was on returning home and getting back to our normal routine. I suggested to Nick that Victoria and I leave within the next few days and he could stay as long as he thought he was needed. He wouldn't hear of Victoria and me going back without him, and he would be ready whenever I wanted.

The only program Bryant and Nick could find on television during that week was a special on Paris. As they watched it, Bryant said he had been there so many times, and that nothing had seemed unusual.

A few days later we decided it was time for us to leave. We had done all we could, and it was up to Bryant to continue his search or find closure and go on with his life. I called to tell him our plans to leave. He had one more request.

"I have something I need to tell you, and I would rather you come alone."

"The three of us have no more secrets. Remember? I will ask Nick and if he agrees, I will come alone."

I hung up the phone. To my surprise Nick was standing behind me.

"If I agree to what?"

"Bryant wants to see me alone."

"Why?"

"I don't know. He said he needs to tell me something and I told him…"

"Yes, I heard. I prefer you not go but that is a decision you have to make. I want you to know that this will be the last time you will ever see him if you decide to go. I've decided that he must be completely out of our lives if our marriage is to continue."

"Are you doubting my love and devotion to you?"

"That's not what I mean. He has a hold on you, and for some reason I feel he will never put you out of his life. I would have never pressed for a friendship with him if I had known your relationship. He isn't Brian. I don't think he meant to hurt you, and maybe he didn't realize you thought he was Brian. I don't have that answer."

Adamantly I said, "Of course he's not Brian."

Nick continued, "In the beginning, I think subconsciously you did believe he was Brian."

Maybe he's right. No. He can't be. Change the subject.

"I've been such a fool. I took you for granted. If our marriage is in danger, and I lose you, I have no one to blame but myself. I'll only go if Bryant agrees to see both of us, and we will tell him our decision never to see him again. If he can't understand or accept that..."

Nick interrupted, "For his sake, I hope he does understand. Go alone. This may be the closure he needs. You seem to have already found yours."

When I arrived, Lynne was leaving. She was very cordial to me, and I could see the concern on her face. If they were to have any future together, I needed to be out of his life forever. I told her good-bye and wished her well. As she opened her car door, I could see her wiping the tears from her eyes. I wanted to run after her and ask her why the tears, but if she had wanted me to know she would have said. She wasn't one to hide her thoughts. I waited until I could no longer see her car before ringing the doorbell.

"Come in. The door's open."

Was this a big mistake? I began to think it was. I wanted to turn and run, but this must be done for his sake, not mine. I slowly walked in. Bryant was still in the wheelchair. He slowly came towards me and motioned for me to sit down. When I did, he gently reached out to take my hand. I remembered his strong hold when I needed comfort. That strength was gone now. He was in constant pain and had a long road ahead for him. I could see the tears as he started.

"Please let me tell you something and don't stop me. Catherine, I

163

have always loved you. I was afraid to tell you because I would lose you. The Westmore men don't have a very good track record when it comes to love. I had to continue my search for my mother. In doing so, I had no idea where my future would take me, and I needed to do it alone. When I saw you had a future — the kind of future you deserved and wanted — I couldn't stand in your way. Being away from you was unbearable at times. I couldn't get you off my mind. I could hear your laughter and see your smiling face. So many times I had reached for the phone to beg you not to leave me and not to marry Nick, but I knew I would fail you. Then when I saw how happy you were, I knew I had made the right decision and so did you. Telling you this now won't change your life, but I wanted you to know I loved you completely. Loving you and being loved by you really did change my life. Just as you realized you could love again and how precious life was, you taught me that also."

"I think all I ever needed to know, and I can't explain why, is that you really did love me. Thank you. For all our sakes, we can never see each other again. You do realize that, don't you?"

"Yes, I do. That is why I need one last time alone with you. I had to tell you that your love wasn't wasted. Nick's a wonderful man. It took a lot of courage on his part to let you come to me after the accident, and even more for him to help me. Thank him again for me."

I got up, walked towards the door and knew that this would be our last meeting. He softly said, "Give me a kiss before you leave."

I turned around and walked over to him, bent down, and softly kissed him. As I gently held his face in my hands, he put his hands on mine. As I drew away, he said, "Just one more." As I began to give him another kiss, I could see that the tears were now gone and that wonderful smile I had always remembered was once again there. I then turned and walked out the door.

I remembered several times when I had to say good-bye to him my tears had blinded me, but this time there were no tears. I knew that there would always be a place in my heart for him and me in his.

Driving away, I remembered seeing Lynne leaving as I arrived.

Had he told her what he had just told me? Was that why she was crying? Would I always stand between them? I would never know the answers now. We both knew that we could never see each other again if my marriage and his future were to succeed.

I drove to Helen's and picked up Nick and Victoria. Nick and I thanked Helen and Reggie for their hospitality during the past weeks. Nick and I had told them everything. There wasn't time to explain my last visit with Bryant. We had to get to the airport. We said our good-byes and left. In my heart I told this little town and all our friends how wonderful it was being part of their lives, but we would never return again. It could be no other way. Without saying a word, Nick knew what I was thinking, and I was sure he felt the same.

On the plane, we sat in silence holding hands. Then Nick put his arms around me and gently held me, and whispered in my ear, "Do you realize that our love is so strong that nothing can ever come between us again?"

"Yes. Do you know how much I really love you now that I am totally free to love you?"

"I always felt that it was Brian who was holding you back and knew that someday you would totally let go, but this really did surprise me. Now I'm truly a part of your life and even your past. I always want to share every moment of your life."

"Believe me. You will. I promise. Oh yes, and by the way, remember that incredible night I promised and delivered? Well, I promised and I will deliver again, I think."

"What are you talking about? Deliver what again?"

"Nick, think about it."

"Deliver, deliver what…? Oh no. You aren't telling me that you're…?"

"You got it, Daddy."

The rest of the trip home was nothing but plans for a new baby. I was almost certain, but needed to confirm it with the doctor. Nick was sure.

When things had settled back into a normal routine at home, I called Helen. I told her what had happened during my last visit with

Bryant. She wasn't at all surprised. She felt very bad that we felt we could never return, but agreed it was the only way things could be. We would always remain friends. We had shared too much to just end this friendship.

CHAPTER 27

The years, as they have a way of doing, passed too quickly. Yes, I had been pregnant and had had a little boy. We named him Nick, Jr., of course. When Helen and Reggie came for little Nick's christening, not one word was mentioned about the past. It was as if all memory had been erased from our minds.

Even though we tried very hard, we were only blessed with the two children. We would have liked at least four, but that was not meant to be.

Dancing lessons for Victoria, riding, and music lessons for the two of them filled our every spare moment. That stuff changed for Nick, Jr., as soon as he was introduced to sports by his father and Uncle Stan.

I was a stay-at-home mom so my children volunteered me for every field trip or class project that needed a mom's help. When asked for volunteers for a Christmas party in the classroom when Nick, Jr., was in the first grade, he volunteered me telling his teacher that his mother didn't do anything and was always available. Living in this small community, most of the women I had met at the children's school were 'just' moms like me. Life couldn't have been better or happier.

I was part of a group that formed a committee to bring culture to our little community. We were always petitioning the city council for appropriations for something. We had worked very hard to get a culture center built and finally succeeded with donations from very generous people who love the arts.

We were given a list of events to consider for the grand opening of our new culture center. I didn't open the pamphlet at the meeting. When I got home, the children were waiting up for me, so I threw it on my desk and went to their rooms. I had forgotten about it until a week later when one of the committee members called to ask my advice about the choices. I promised her to read it later in the day and get back with her.

By the time I got the kids off to school, Nick off to work, the laundry done and the house picked up, it was time for lunch. I sat down with a sandwich and a cup of coffee and picked up the pamphlet. Right then Nick called and said he had to fly to London and asked if I would I start packing for him. So I threw the pamphlet back on the desk and forgot about it for the next few days. Nick hated traveling and didn't unless it was absolutely necessary. With Nick gone, there wasn't any time for reading unless it was to the children. I forgot about my promise.

Nick had been gone for a week. When it was time for him to come home, the children wanted to bake Daddy a cake, make a 'welcome home' banner, and fix his favorite dinner. Since they were in school all day, the plans were left up to me. They knew I could handle it with little or no help from them. I simply put everything else on hold and took care of the festivities at hand. Nick and the children told me I had as usual, outdone myself. Since that plane ride home, so many years ago, I spent every day of my life showing Nick my love.

By the time I remembered about the pamphlet, the committee was meeting again to make a final decision. Because of our homecoming plans for Nick, I couldn't attend the meeting and decided to go along with any decisions they made.

A week later I opened the newspaper to the local news. Big headlines, "Sensational New Artist, Bryant, Invited To Open Culture Center." It continued with a little of his accomplishments and life. I read the article but quickly forgot what I had read. My mind was not on what I was reading. All I could think was, why after so many years? He knew we lived here. The article didn't mention if he was married and if he had children.

I quickly went to my desk and started looking through the pile of papers for the pamphlet I had failed to read. I opened it and continued reading. There was one brief paragraph about a new artist simply known as "Bryant".

I had always placed the newspaper on the table next to Nick's favorite chair. That evening after dinner, he sat down expecting to reach for the newspaper. "Where's tonight's paper?"

"Before you read the paper, we need to talk."

He laughed and said, "Don't tell me that you've been so busy that you forgot to pay the paper boy, and he stopped delivery the paper. I'm just teasing. What's up and where's my paper?"

I explained how I hadn't had time to read the material given me or attend the meetings, and I had no idea that Bryant had been selected to open our culture center.

"Well, if you would have known, what excuse would you have used to reject him as a possibility? It seems that the committee was unanimous on their decision. Don't worry about it. Enough time has passed that I'm sure time has healed all wounds. Well, that is the old saying anyway. Are you really uncomfortable about this?"

"No. Not at all. I was afraid you would be after my last visit and conversation with Bryant."

"See, I told you that you always worry before there's something to worry about. Since he seems to have made a success of his artistic life, maybe he has done so with his personal life also."

"It would be nice to know if he had continued his search for his mother. Wouldn't it be nice if they found each other after all these years?"

"Catherine, there you go again. Now you won't be satisfied until you know how that little drama has evolved. Am I right?"

"Well, you know that his story was pretty interesting and intriguing. He should write his autobiography."

"He is an artist, not a writer. Maybe he has his life in his paintings. Remember the one that looked like you? Was it supposed to be his grandmother or mother? She did resemble you a little."

"I don't remember what, if any, explanation he had."

Was Nick hiding his true thoughts about Bryant entering our lives again?

"Nick, tell me how you want me to handle this, and I will. I can tell the committee I really can't help on this project and stay away. I don't want to do anything that would hurt you. It has been a long time. Apparently he has made a new life for himself. When he accepted the invitation, maybe he had forgotten that we live here."

"You know, Catherine, so far you have handled this situation very well, and I trust your judgement."

"Thanks for the vote of confidence."

Nick was right. I really wanted to know how Bryant's life had been and if he had found his mother or had given up. I could handle seeing him again, but I wasn't sure how he would feel. *If he does remember that we live here, why did he accept the invitation? We agreed that we could never see each other again.* I was curious if Lynne was still in the picture. I was sure all my questions would be answered very soon.

I attended the committee meeting at the culture center and offered my help, apologizing that my time would be limited because the kids were involved in so much those days. They also knew that with Nick doing a little more traveling, it would be hard for me to get away in the evenings.

The paintings began to arrive, and I found myself at the culture center more often than I had planned. Bryant would not be arriving until all the paintings were there. He had insisted on arranging them personally. I declined being on the welcoming committee.

Bryant arrived on the same day that the last painting did. Several days after all the festivities honoring him had begun — which we didn't attend — I went to the center to get a view of the paintings. I knew that afternoon he would be at one of those luncheons and wouldn't be at the culture center. It wasn't open, but I had my own key.

I entered the room, and suddenly all the memories came rushing back. The old paintings from the "Winter Beach" collection and new ones were intermingled. It was as if he had put his life on canvas but in no specific order.

The paintings he had copied from those of his mother that had been destroyed were there, much to my surprise. He chose to conceal the true nature of their origin. They were all grouped together with the heading above them, "Not of My World". I knew that would really confuse everyone, but not me.

The one from the "Winter Beach" collection that he had explained to us with the snow and the blanket still had not been named. I remembered that he had not put a name on it the first time he showed it also. A bench was placed in front of it. As I sat there, I could hear his voice telling me once again what he had felt as he painted it. So many memories came back. Some I wanted to remember, and some I had tried so hard to forget. The memory I tried and thought I had succeeded to forget was how much I had loved him. How different my life would have been if I had known he loved me.

How long I sat there, I don't know. My eyes were filling with tears that began running down my cheeks. I wanted to run as fast and as far as possible from this place, but I couldn't move. The past began to overtake the present. The sensation of his arms around me, and his lips on mine was too real. I didn't want the past to take over. No. No. I couldn't go through this again. I had come so far and was so sure the past was buried so deeply that it would never resurface. I jumped up and began to run out of the room. As I approached the doorway, Bryant stepped out of the shadows. I ran right into his open arms. He held me so tightly, I couldn't get out of his embrace, and I didn't try as he kissed me with all the passion I had remembered.

"I have been watching you for the past hour. Do you realize how long you have been sitting here? Catherine, we can't hide or deny this love we have any longer. The years have not stolen that from us."

"No. I can't love you. I have gone through so much to stop. I could never understand the hold you had on me, but I have let go. I can't do this to Nick. He has been my whole life, and we have a family. You and I had our chance. Yes, you are right. No matter how hard I try, I can't forget. You once asked me how I could love two men equally, and I still don't have an answer. I honestly don't know which one of you I would have chosen if you had told me that you loved me at the beginning. At one time I would have given anything to…"

He didn't let me finish the sentence. He held me tighter and said, "We can have what we both wanted so many years ago. I have dreamed of holding you and making love to you from the very beginning. We both want this."

I broke loose from his arms and ran. As I was running, I heard him say, "I will love you forever. Someday you will come to me, and I will be waiting."

I yelled, as I ran away, "No. That will never happen."

I got into my car and drove directly home. When I arrived home, Nick was there and had let the sitter go.

"Where have you been? I've been worried. The sitter said you left hours ago. I started dinner."

I just looked at him and knew it was time for secrets again. This time no matter what I had to do, it will always remain a secret.

"Years ago, we agreed that Bryant could never be a part of our lives. So I went to the culture center alone today and looked at his paintings. No one was there because of the luncheon. They were magnificent. He will truly earn his place in the art world. Even though he doesn't need the fortune, the fame will certainly fulfill him."

"Catherine, I know what I said, but I really would like to take the children and see the exhibit for ourselves. They have been so excited to meet him and told their classmates that their parents personally know the artist. Victoria told everyone about that little card he painted for her before she was born. I respect your decision not to join us, but don't disappoint the kids. Think it over. I hope you will come too."

"You and the kids will love it as much as I did. It would be wrong of me to say you guys can't go. I will think about it."

I did think it over and decided that what Bryant needed was to see me with my family. I hoped he would remember his life without his mother and know how much my children needed me in their lives. When I told Nick I would be going with them, he gave me that 'I know what your are up to' look.

"You just want to find out how his life is going. Maybe his mother will be there. But most important, can you get past your last visit?"

Nick was referring to the last visit in Michigan. I was referring to the one that day.

"Yes. I can."

"Remember, he was very vulnerable the last time you saw him. He went through a lot, and you were the one that really pulled him through. He might have confused love with gratitude."

"As usual, sweetheart, you're probably right. Don't you ever get tired of being right?"

He grabbed me in his arms, picked me up, and said, "No, I made the right decision when I asked you to be my wife, and I haven't been able to do anything wrong since."

Boy, I wish I could say the same. Nick seems to make even the worst situation seem not as bad.

CHAPTER 28

The next two days flew by as if I had gone to sleep and woke up two days later. It was time for the formal opening of the culture center. As the four of us prepared to leave the house I went over to the TV to turn it off. The news was just beginning and reporters and admiring fans surrounded Bryant. He had started to speak when a note was handed to him.

"I am so sorry, but I need to leave immediately for personal reasons. I wanted so much to share this with you. Thank you for giving me the chance to share my life with you through my paintings. I hope to return before the exhibit closes. Please come and enjoy yourselves. My thoughts will be with all of you."

As much as I hated to admit it, I was disappointed. He needed to see me with my children. But now I could go to the exhibit with my family knowing he wouldn't be there.

When we arrived at the center, everyone was still talking about Bryant's sudden departure. What was so important that he had to leave immediately? No one knew what the note said. No one recognized the man who had given it to him. I tried to find out if Lynne accompanied him on the trip. Everyone agreed that he had come alone and left alone. Having his own private jet, he had left immediately after the press interview. We did manage to find out from a friend of a friend, who had an acquaintance working at the airport, that the plane was headed for Michigan.

It was hard for me to concentrate on the paintings, which I had already seen. Nick and the children were too busy admiring each one to notice my agony at first, but then Nick said, "Well, my little detective, I'm willing to bet the farm on Helen getting a call as soon as we get home."

"As soon as I get home. I'm leaving now. You guys enjoy the

show. I've seen it, remember."

"Okay, Sherlock, how do you propose we get home if you are leaving now?"

"Right. Well I left my cell home. Do you have yours?"

"Yes, but…"

"Nick, quit teasing, and just give me the phone, please."

I knew he was just as interested as I was. I didn't want to be interrupted, so I went to the car to make the call. You might know Helen's line was busy. Maybe she was getting the info from one of her friends. When I finally had gotten through, I told her what had happened. She had heard nothing except that someone was on the island already, but no one paid any attention to it.

"You're right, Catherine. There was some talk about an exhibit in New York. When he's on the island, he never leaves or has company. He has a handyman that takes care of the grounds and comes to the mainland for supplies."

"Well, he was here but isn't any longer."

"Catherine, how long has he been there?"

"The past four days."

"Four days? That's about the time we noticed lights on the island, and we thought he had moved back. I could call Lynne, but I'm sure she doesn't know anything. Talk is that whatever may have been going on between them has ended. I told you long ago that he was too mysterious."

"Don't be silly, Helen. There is a reasonable explanation to all of this."

"Yes, and I'm sure you will find out what it is. It has been a long time. Are you sure you want to get involved in his life again?"

Since I didn't know what to say, there were a few moments of silence on my end.

"Catherine, why are you hesitating to answer me? Is there something you're not telling me?"

"No. I was thinking. I'm leaving it up to you to find out all you can. Even though Nick and I could never continue a friendship with Bryant, we had always wanted Bryant to become a successful artist and someday find his mother. I'll talk to Nick and see what he thinks. Maybe he will be interested enough to suggest we look into it ourselves."

"You do just that and give me a call back. I kinda think you must be watching too much television or reading too many mysteries. What mystery could there possibly be here? You're making too much out of this."

I went back into the exhibit. Nick and the kids were still very engrossed in the paintings.

I was anxious to tell Nick the little that I had learned. I asked them, "Are you ready to leave?"

They all answered together, "Absolutely not. We haven't begun to enjoy this."

Victoria was very disappointed about not being able to meet Bryant. We told her we were sure she would someday. After all, he did say he would try to return. Nick promised that if he did return, he would make certain she got to meet him personally. That satisfied her. Nick felt slighted because he hadn't gotten a painting like Victoria had. We explained that it had been years since we had seen Bryant, and he didn't know that we had a little boy too. I looked at Nick and saw the look on his face that said, "Don't be too sure of that. We don't really know that he doesn't know."

He turned to the children and said, "I'll tell you what I am going to do. Both of you discuss what painting is your favorite and I will buy it for you. How does that sound? Then we will all have an original to enjoy."

Victoria asked, "Do we have to decide tonight, Dad?"

"No. Take your time. This is something that we will keep forever, so don't make a hasty decision. Your mother and I will put our vote in, but the final decision will be yours."

"Thanks. You are the best dad a kid could have," they chimed in unison. They looked at each other and ran over to Nick and hugged him very tightly.

At that moment I couldn't help but wish with all my heart that Bryant could have witnessed this scene. I was sure he would walk out of our lives forever. I knew him well enough to know that he couldn't or wouldn't destroy this family no matter what the personal cost to him.

The ride home was an endless session of mind changing. The children realized that their father had given them a much harder decision to make than they had realized. If it hadn't been for them, the ride home would have been in silence. I tried to change the subject and get Nick to respond, but he just drove quietly without showing any emotion at all. I began to get the uneasy feeling that I was losing something and couldn't stop it.

When we got home Victoria said, "Mom. Dad. Nick and I decided we would like the painting not named."

I told them, "That is the only one not for sale. There was a little note at the side of the painting. It read, 'I can share all the paintings of my life with you, except this one'."

Nick had seen the note and hadn't realized that the children hadn't seen it. He said, "You two were so busy trying to decide what painting you wanted, you obviously didn't see the note."

The evening had been so full of excitement for the children that they were very tired, and they wanted to go directly to bed. I wanted to sit a while and talk. Victoria said, "We did all the talking on the way home. I guess we can listen to what you have to say."

I said, "That's okay. What I have to say can wait. It's late and you have school tomorrow."

Victoria said, "You and Dad were very quiet. Is something wrong? If you have changed your mind about buying a painting, that's okay with us. We know that's a lot of money to spend."

Nick put his arms around both children. "No. That's not it. I really do want you children to have the painting of your choice. Mom and I will agree to the one you pick. Now we all have had quite a big evening, and it's time for bed."

I watched Nick as he held the children close to him. He stood there for a few minutes, and I could see his eyes filling with tears. Victoria looked at him and said, "Dad, what's wrong? Are you crying?"

"Honey, I'm fine. I was just thinking how lucky I am to have the two of you."

Then to put them at ease, he stood back, looked at them, and snickered, "You know, of course, that buying a painting just wiped out your college fund. I guess both of you will have to get a job?"

Nick, Jr., quickly replied, "No problem, Dad. We'll put Mom to work."

Nick looked at me for the first time since we had left the culture center with a half smile and said, "Seriously, I don't think that's going to happen. Who will take care of us? You both know that the three of us would be lost without her."

My heart was breaking because I knew what he really meant by that remark. I couldn't wait until the children were tucked in bed, and we could talk. Every moment that passed was pushing us further apart.

We got ready for bed in silence. Something we had never done. Each was waiting for the other to start the conversation, neither knowing how. Finally, as we lay in bed, I turn and put my arms around him and said, "Please talk to me. We have never been as far apart as we are at this moment, and it frightens me."

He turned towards me with such sadness in his voice and said, "Please let me try to explain how I feel and don't say anything until I finish. I was sure that he was out of our lives forever when we left Michigan because you had felt you owed him something and that you had repaid him. When he told you how much you really had meant to him and how much he really loved and still loves you, I thought I could live with that, knowing you didn't love him. I don't think now that he is willing to ever let you go. Seeing our children so enchanted with him even though they have never met him also frightens me. When you had those moments that you couldn't let me into your private world, I thought I was dealing with the memory of Brian. I knew I could deal with that. I think you really thought when you first met Bryant and no one knew about his existence, that you convinced yourself that he was Brian. I think if you would have continued your sessions with Dr. Sterling that you would have realized that yourself. In the beginning Bryant was there to help you and then when you fell in love with him, he was Brian. He wanted to be Brian. Honey, keep Brian in a little corner of your heart. That is his space, but take Bryant out of there. There isn't enough room for both of them. They are not one in the same. Honey, you or something about you, is in every one of his paintings. You had to realize that. I wish I had never made that promise to the children about buying them a painting, but a promise is a promise."

His voice started to crack, and I knew he couldn't continue. He was now holding me tightly; and we were both crying.

"What have I done to you? I should have never told you my secret and I should have never gone to Bryant. I know now that I should have told Helen I was sorry to hear about the accident and stayed away. I think you're right. I never got over the fact that I wasn't by Brian's side at the end. I wasn't there to ease his pain or hold him and he died alone. I knew that Bryant might die and now I realize I didn't want him to die alone. I needed to be there if he did. I couldn't let Brian die alone again. I had to be…Oh my God! What did I just say? Nick, I need to see Dr. Sterling again."

"May I go with you this time? I think we both need his help now. It has been ignored long enough. We can do this together."

"Together. That is the most beautiful word you could have spoken at this moment."

We just held each other, and our tears became tears of joy and hope. We were both emotionally drained and found sleep came very quickly.

The next morning everything was back to normal with the children. Nick, Jr., had a hard time getting up, and Victoria couldn't decide what top to wear with what shoes. Nick remarked that she reminded him of me in the early days when we were dating. He told her that I had to have shoes to match every outfit I owned.

"Nothing has changed. Check your mom's closet."

I looked at Nick and said, "So, I like shoes. It could be worse. I could like diamonds. Come to think of it, I do, but I don't have one for each outfit."

Nick thought for a moment and said, "On second thought, Catherine, you can have all the shoes you want."

As we watched the children get on the school bus, I picked up the phone and made an appointment with Dr. Sterling. When I explained the situation, he was more than willing to see us later that day. He always left a couple hours a day free in case of emergencies, such as a golf date or tennis match. I guess his sense of humor was one of the reasons he made his patients feel so at ease.

The session went very well. Dr. Sterling agreed that to me Bryant was Brian. He wasn't sure why Bryant chose to let me believe that he was Brian. Without personally knowing Bryant, he really couldn't answer that. He said, "With his living on the island long before anyone found him there —and that was you, Catherine— he did appear mysterious when he wouldn't tell you his name at first. Think back on the first two visits you made to the island. You must admit it did start out like a good mystery story. I also think that you blame yourself for Brian's death because you weren't by his side. You couldn't have saved him, from what you told me earlier. It's time to let go. Stop blaming yourself."

We accomplished a lot in that first session. Dr. Sterling agreed that Nick and I should continue the sessions together. Nick needed to know everything with no secrets.

The exhibit was a huge success. We couldn't understand why, but the children for their own reasons, decided that they didn't need an original painting. Nick assured them he was joking about it being their college fund, but they convinced us that wasn't the reason. They knew he had been kidding, talked it over, and that was their decision. We didn't question it.

Bryant never did return during the exhibit. The unsold paintings were sent back to Michigan. That didn't surprise me. He had made the island his home now. The note, the man that delivered it, and the decision not to return, were as usual a mystery that still surrounded him. All of this soon became part of our past. A past now that was really just that. I had informed Helen of what had happened and she was so relieved. She declared she would never let me know anything about the island or its occupants again.

With my curious nature, that word, 'occupants' started me thinking. My imagination started working overtime. As famous as Bryant had become, I was sure we would be reading about him in the paper someday or seeing him on the nightly news. But several years passed and nothing. He seemed to have disappeared from public life altogether. We waited, thinking that a new exhibit would emerge at any time. But none did.

CHAPTER 29

Raising our children was all that mattered. When it came time for Victoria to go off to college, we wondered where the time had gone. We had been so much involved in our children's lives that we had no regrets and so many wonderful memories.

Our marriage had survived a lot of unpleasant events and it was stronger for what we had faced together. But the fact that we finally faced them together was the real reason for its success. From the day of our last session with Dr. Sterling, Bryant was never an issue and never discussed. For me there were no more dreams or doubts.

The only dreams Nick and I had, we shared. They were for our future, and hopefully a future filled with grandchildren.

Ann and Stan had gotten their family. They had adopted twin boys and a girl. Our children grew up together and are still the best of friends. I never told Ann about Bryant, and she never asked. All that time, she stood by me asking no questions. I once wrote her a little note to express my gratitude. It read:

True friends are hard to come by, and yet I found one in you. No matter what I say or do, you do not judge me falsely and always understand when I have a problem or need a helping hand. Thank you for your friendship and always being there. At least I know, if nothing else, you will always care.

I also sent it off to Helen and Reggie. It had more meaning for them because they did know and keep my secret. Even when they knew Nick knew, they never discussed that visit during the accident with anyone. They never judged me and tried very hard to understand. If they didn't fully understand, they didn't say. Reggie's company offered him a great job in the Chicago area, and he accepted. We were then able to visit them often. They kept their boat in Michigan and stayed in touch with all the old friends.

We never returned to Michigan.

As Victoria was preparing to leave for college, she came to my room one evening and wanted to talk. We had our little mother-daughter talks quite often. I would miss that when she was at college. She came in and handed me the little picture Bryant had slipped in my pocket so many years ago.

"Mom, I don't know what happened that night at the opening of our culture center, but I do know it had something to do with the artist and this picture. I remember the silence on our way home and knew something was very wrong between you and Dad. Nick and I talked about it and that was why we didn't want another painting in our home. After you left my room that night, I took this picture and wanted to destroy it, but it was so beautiful I couldn't, so I put it away and vowed never to bring it out again. When everything between you and Dad was fine again, I was sure it was because the picture was out of sight, but still didn't know the connection. I do know that someday I hope to have a perfect marriage like the two of you. I must admit that I had forgotten all about this until I found it today in a red velvet box you had given me for Valentine's Day years ago."

With the painting in my hand, I found it hard to look down at it. Finally I did. Quite surprised, there were no tears. In fact, there was no emotion except admiring a beautiful painting. I looked up. Standing behind Victoria in the doorway, was Nick.

"How long have you been standing there?"

"Long enough to know that you can tell her the story now. The years and our understanding have made it a beautiful story."

"Are you sure you want to hear this again?"

"Yes, and I'll be here to help you to help her understand."

Together we told her the whole story, even the fact that I loved this man very much and still couldn't understand how I could have loved him and her father equally.

"You will love many times in your life, but you will be able to decide what true love is when it comes along. When you do, remember no secrets. When I had met Bryant, I had recently lost the man I thought would always be by my side, and the loneliness was unbearable. Bryant made me realize that life does go on. I'm sure now that he didn't mean to complicate my life. He wanted me in a world with just the two of us. When I met and fell in love with your father, I realized I needed more than the island and Bryant's world. I'm so glad I made the right decision because if I hadn't none of us would be sitting here having this conversation."

"Mom, I gotta tell you. I'm glad you did too."

The three of us were laughing and talking, and knew that these little talks would soon be very few and far between.

"Just one more question, Mom. What ever happened to him? Does he still paint and live on that island?"

Nick answered that one. "We don't know. With all his accomplishments we felt he had a great future but he seemed to vanish. If he is still painting, nothing has been exhibited, to our knowledge since the show that you saw. Your mother wanted to believe that the note was from his mother, and that the mystery man that handed him the note was a private detective that had found her. So I agreed that was a very good ending for him. He had what he had always wanted and I had my wife back forever."

"Dad, that was so sweet, and Mom, you have such an imagination. I've always said you should be a writer. Why don't you write a novel? I'm sure you could really make a mystery out of his search."

"I just might do that."

The following morning Helen called. She had just gotten a call from Mae in Michigan. Bryant had died, and the funeral was being held on the island.

Nick and I decided that we could face this and would attend. We didn't know what to expect after all those years. When we arrived at the island, we found that he hadn't lived there solely for the past several years. There were many people we didn't know. A lot of the town's people were there. Mae was there. She had always liked Bryant. I had to ask her, "Mae, will Lynne be attending the funeral?"

"I can't say. She left years ago and never returned. Elaine finally sold the business and stayed here until she passed away two years ago. We all figured Bryant was the reason Lynne left. Elaine was so devastated when Lynne left that we never asked questions."

The funeral was very simple. Bryant had requested to be buried on his beloved island. As we sat at the gravesite listening to a fellow artist giving the eulogy, we were having our own pleasant memories. I reached down and picked a tiny white flower, remembering the day he had picked them and gently placed them in my hair. I could feel his hand touching mine and see his wonderful smile. I heard that velvet voice now silenced forever. I put him in another corner of my heart a corner reserved for only him.

Nick whispered, "Are you all right? It's okay to cry. I understand."

"I'll be okay."

The gentleman giving the eulogy asked if anyone had anything to say. Everyone was silent. He continued, "Most of you already know that the last years of Bryant's life were stolen from him by a muscular disease. Actually his life ended when he could no longer paint. His last exhibit sadly was years ago in a little town in up state New York. He knew then that he would never paint again. But we won't dwell on that. We all had the opportunity to know him, love him, and are inspired by his wonderful paintings. He was a very private person and his paintings revealed that. Feel free after the service to go into the lighthouse and see them again. Stay as long as you like. Thank you all for coming. I'm sure Bryant is watching us and once again is able to paint this, his last scene."

As we all walked past the casket for one final farewell, and oh how many times had I needed that last good-bye, I leaned down and whispered, "I know you would ask for just one more kiss good-bye."

I gently pressed my lips against the casket. Nick held my arm, giving me the support I needed now from him.

Nick knew I couldn't go into the cottage or the lighthouse and didn't suggest we do. If it had changed, I didn't want to know. I needed to keep my memories of the first time I had entered it because I had learned to treasure those days and not to fear them.

As we were walking back to the dock to return to the mainland, a woman came out of the cottage carrying a painting. She was elderly, but carried herself like a queen. The years had been kind to her. Her beauty emerging through her lined face. She must have been watching from inside and had chosen not to join the mourners for some reason. She walked over to me, handed me the unnamed painting, and said, "He wanted you to have this."

In shock I said, "How do you know who I am?"

"I'm his mother."

Speechless, Nick and I watched the woman walk away from us. I stood there clutching the painting, stunned, with the words 'I am his mother' burning in my mind. Unable to speak or move, I could feel Nick's arms around me holding me up. She didn't turn around to look back as she walked back into the cottage. Nick didn't need to ask. He led me towards the cottage. We both needed to see and talk to her. Maybe she didn't want to talk to me otherwise she wouldn't have just walked away. Did we dare intrude on her sorrow and at this time? How much time had she had with her son?

The door to the cottage was open and guests were coming and going. I stood at the door remembering the first time I had entered it. I can still see the windows covered with years of weather. Today they were covered with black drapes.

Slowly walking in was like walking into the past. Everything was as I remembered. He hadn't changed a thing. His presence was very strong. I pictured him standing in that room as he had so many years ago. There was a sudden surge of happiness and then sadness. The happiness I felt when I was with him and the sadness when I would leave. There had been so many years of that feeling until it all finally ended for me. The years of loving him seemed so long ago as I reflected on the good times and feelings.

I looked around for the woman, but she was nowhere to be seen. I walked over to the door that I thought might lead to the lighthouse and tried to open it. It was locked. I couldn't help but wonder who had locked it, Bryant or his mother. So many locked doors that obviously were too painful to open, but for whom?

Behind me I heard, "You're probably right. That door should be unlocked."

I turned around to see Elizabeth with a key in her hand. She walked over to the door, hesitated, and turned to me and said, "I think you should be the one to unlock it. I locked it when my son died. Locked doors seem to be a tradition in this family. One that needs to be broken forever."

Without thinking or asking Nick how he felt about this, I took the key. As I put it into the lock, I could feel the tears beginning to fill my eyes. I slowly turned the key, opened the door, and saw all the paintings he had copied of his mother's. Next to each copy was the damaged original.

I looked behind me and realized that the door was closed. Elizabeth and I stood there alone. I could see the empty spot on the wall where she had removed the painting she had given me. Above was a plaque that read, "She gave me life, and you gave me a reason to live."

I was wishing Nick had stayed with us. I asked Elizabeth if she minded if Nick joined us, and she said, "Of course not. I opened the door. Nick was standing across the room talking to Mae. I motioned for him to join us. Slowly he walked towards me and whispered softly, "This is a very private time for his mother and you. I'll be here when you're finished."

"There are no more secrets. I want you with me."

He took my hand and followed me into the lighthouse, but suddenly turned to me and said, "I had everything he couldn't, including the only woman he loved. So now I am giving Elizabeth and you a chance to share his love together."

Elizabeth walked over to Nick and took his hand, "I think you would like to know what I am about to tell your wife. Please join us."

Putting his arm around her, the three of us walked to the steps of the lighthouse.

Seeing the contentment on her face, I had to know, "How long have you been back in his life?"

"I have been with Bryant since his last exhibit in New York. I had seen an article in a magazine about a new aspiring American artist.

There was a picture of him standing next to one of his paintings. I knew that it was one I had painted many years ago. The article mentioned that he was living on an island in Michigan. The message he received that night in New York was from me. I didn't think he would leave without opening the culture center with his exhibit. I thought I had at least a week at the lighthouse to collect my thoughts and that I would be well prepared to meet him. When he arrived within hours, I wasn't ready and resigned myself to accept whatever would be. It only to took minutes before we were hugging and crying together."

I asked, "When did you realize Bryant was searching for you?"

"I had known for years. I had been so ashamed of what I had done and my past, that I couldn't face him. I was certain that he hated me, and I couldn't understand why he was trying to find me. I was afraid of what he would say when he did. Quite a few years after I deserted my family— today I think the phrase is, 'trying to find myself'— I decided that my place was with them. My husband had the means to keep me out of their lives completely. I tried to follow Bryant's life, but his father kept him out of the public eye. I only read about my husband's great financial success. I still have a few articles and pictures I managed to find about Bryant in an occasional paper or magazine. I tried to reach Bryant and wrote to him many times. My letters were never returned or answered so I knew Bryant had received them and didn't want me in his life now."

Not at all surprised, I asked, "The letters that Bryant thought had been from a school in France were from you?"

"Yes."

"He told Nick and me about them. He wondered if they had been from you. His father convinced him that they weren't."

"Yes, I know. He was torn between devotion to his father and the need to find me. His father deserved the devotion, and I deserved nothing."

Nick was very quiet. Naturally, I wasn't. "No. You didn't deserve to be separated from your son for so many years just because your husband couldn't forgive you. Bryant was ready to forgive you at any point in his life."

Elizabeth smiled at me and said, "You would know that because you knew him better than anyone did from what he told me. He knew about his illness when he met you. He didn't know how slowly or quickly it would progress. He knew he couldn't let you go through losing him as you did Brian. He told me that he loved you from the first moment he saw you. Then as your friendship evolved into love, he knew how devastated you would be when he had to leave you. He felt he was taking Brian's place. So you see when he would become very distant during those days you spent together on the island, that was the only way he could spare you from his fate. He told me all about your long talks. I'm happy to say we also had time to get to know each other especially when he no longer had the use of his arms or legs. At least his mind was never affected. We could talk for hours at a time. While he was still able to walk and travel, he visited me often at my villa in France. Then the visits became less frequent. At first I couldn't bear to visit the island, but when it became harder for him to travel, I would come to him. He didn't want anyone to know about his illness. My visits were kept a secret. I needed to love and care for my son as much as he needed his mother's love and care. There were many times I wanted to call you, Catherine, and ask you to come and try to comfort him. He wouldn't allow it. You had given him his life back after the accident. He didn't want you to see him as he was."

I couldn't help but wonder. Was that the real reason he wouldn't let her call me? Or was it because of our last meeting?

"Did he tell you about our last meeting?"

"The day you left to go back home after the accident?"

Because of her question, I had the feeling that she knew what meeting I was referring to, but she wasn't sure if I had told Nick about it.

"Yes. He was so overcome with the knowledge of what was ahead for him that all he could think about was having you by his side. He then realized how selfish he was for only thinking of himself and not you and your family. He regretted what he had done by admitting so adamantly his love for you at that last meeting. But he also knew that you were so much in love with Nick and you had a family; neither of which he could bear to destroy. So he held you in his heart tenderly until the end."

She took hold of my hands, like Bryant had done, and tearfully continued, "Bryant told me that if he had told you, soon after he had met you, about his illness, he knew you would have stayed with him. You would have lost your chance of happiness with Nick. He had to make a choice, and he did. He wanted you to have the life and family you deserved and had always wanted. That was something that was impossible for him to give you. Look at your family and your life, and tell me he made the wrong choice."

She knew what my answer would be. "No. He didn't. Knowing the truth would have made my life easier. I would have understood and not spent so many years loving him and wondering why he couldn't love me or anyone else. I never stopped loving him as a friend, but I had to let go. Don't misunderstand, I do love my husband very much. I, too, had to make a choice. Nick loved me and let me know it every moment we were together and Bryant couldn't. I knew I had to walk away, and I did. Bryant had made me realize I could love again and find happiness."

I knew it was difficult for Elizabeth to continue, but she did. "His love for you and knowing that you once loved him, sustained him until the end, except for one brief setback. He had made a difficult decision. We were sitting on the beach at the island, and he started talking about you."

"Mother, I wish I could hold Catherine in my arms one more time. I want to feel her lips on mine, her hand holding mine, but that's impossible now. I couldn't bear to see her knowing I could never feel her touch or any touch again. I can't live like this any longer and decided euthanasia is the only answer for me now."

"Bryant, please don't mention that. Death isn't the answer. You can still hold her in your mind and heart. Please let me call her."

"No. She can't know about this. I couldn't bear to see the pity on her face. I refused her love, and now I don't want her pity. You can't imagine the pain of holding her in my mind and heart and not being able to hold her in my arms. You can never know that feeling."

"Yes I can. I held you in my mind and heart for many years. At times the feeling was so unbearable that I wanted to die. I kept the hope alive that someday I would be able to. You didn't refuse her love. You spared her your fate. That was a greater love and sacrifice. You're right. There's no way I could understand or feel your pain. Remember and cherish all the precious moments you were able to experience."

"There was a difference. You knew you would be able to...Let's end this conversation. I want you to help me make the arrangements or I will find someone who will."

"Catherine, I could hear the pain and anger in his voice and wanted to help him, but couldn't. I wanted to keep him close to me as long as possible. I told him I would consider it, but had no intention of doing so. I needed time to convince him that he needed to see you, especially since I knew the end would be coming sooner than he anticipated. I had hoped that seeing you would make him fight to survive a little longer and give us more time together."

Even though Elizabeth's last weeks with her son were so painful, she cherished every moment that they had spent together. She managed a smile and said, "It was his wish to end his days here. He wanted to visit the villa one more time. We stayed there for a week. I brought him back to the island a few weeks before the end. Here he could feel your presence. It gave him peace. I was able to avoid the decision he had made. I could tell by his face that he was happy and content. Come walk with me to the top of the lighthouse."

We followed her to the very top. There situated in the center of the room was a portrait of me, unfinished. He had painted it from memory. He had started to paint a sunset in the background. Elizabeth continued, "He tried so hard to finish it, but couldn't. It took him two years to complete what you see there. Now you know how I recognized you. You look exactly like he remembered you. Someday it will be yours, but right now I can't part with any of his paintings. The only reason I gave that one to you was because he made me promise that if you came to the funeral I would personally give it to you. Can you find it in your heart to forgive him for the sadness he caused in your life?"

"I forgave him many years ago when I realized myself that I wanted him to be Brian. I even thought at one point that he was Brian and had come back to help me love again and to tell me good-bye. Brian didn't have a chance to say good-bye. Now I realize why each time we were together Bryant would always leave me with a 'good-bye' and a kiss."

I began to cry, and Nick put his arms around me to comfort me. We looked at Elizabeth and saw the sorrow that she was experiencing. Nick turned to me.

"I know you're fine. I think someone needs to be comforted more than you."

I smiled and slipped out of his arms. He walked over to Elizabeth and gently took her in his arms.

We left the island knowing that Elizabeth would be returning to her family in France. She had remarried and had two daughters. Bryant had finally become part of his mother's life and part of a family. She was so thankful for having her son in her life again. Even with the sadness of his last years, her life was complete. We knew as we parted that we would never meet again.

Printed in the United States
R182000001B/R1820PG13031D012B/12